Sinful Cinderella

Cover art by Anita Valle

http://www.anitavalleart.com

ISBN-13: 978-1518811968
ISBN-10: 1518811965

Printed in the USA

First Edition, September 2015

Sinful Cinderella

by Anita Valle

www.anitavalleart.com

Prologue

That prince is *mine.*

Not yet, of course. But I'll get him. *And* his castle. *And* his kingdom! Mine. Then I'll flaunt my victory in my stepsisters' faces, rub their crooked noses in it. But they won't get to taste my wealth, not a crumb.

Trouble is, I can't do it until I've saved enough white magic. And to do that, I have to be *good.*

I hate being good.

Chapter I

Stepmother summons me to the sitting room.

She's tried to persuade me to call her Mother. Or Countess. Or even Elira, her given name. I persist with Stepmother. A reminder to her and to me of what she truly is: an object to be stepped on.

Once I have enough white magic, I'll crush her like a beetle beneath my heel. Crunch, crunch, crunch will go her bones.

I enter the sitting room which is mostly white. The lace curtains, the velvet furniture, the plush carpet. I think Stepmother chose white because it shows every speck of dirt so splendidly. There's always a spot for me to scrub out somewhere.

"Hello, my darling," Stepmother says. Though she treats me like a servant, she insists on calling me 'darling' like her daughters. Probably revenge for my calling her Stepmother. I promise you, I'm nobody's darling.

She holds a long sheet of parchment in her brittle fingers. The bottom of it curls upward and I notice the royal seal at the bottom. It's from the king.

"It seems," Stepmother says, "that the prince is giving a ball."

"Oh," I say, perfectly respectful. But really I want to say, so? The prince can't go a season without a ball or two. He's a party mongrel.

Stepmother taps the parchment with her finger. "This one is interesting. He has requested that all the unmarried young ladies of the kingdom attend."

"Unmarried?" My fingertips tingle. "Does that mean I may go too?"

Stepmother lifts her pigeon-gray eyes to me. Amused. Disdainful. She doesn't have to say a word.

Of course I'm not going.

"Now," she says, "my daughters will need gowns for this ball. New gowns, naturally. Something... striking... and sure to entice the prince." She smiles coldly at me. "You have three days."

My stomach pinches. "Three days?" To sew two ball gowns from scratch? Buying the cloth, selecting a design, cutting the pieces, sewing-sewing-sewing, and then the fittings, adjustments, revisions while my stepsisters fuss and fidget. I need a month to make those gowns.

"In addition to your other chores, of course," Stepmother says.

I don't trust my voice so I merely nod.

Stepmother stands, rolling the parchment. "You should buy the cloth now before the best pieces are snatched up. Oh... and when you return, I notice there's a smudge of something on the arm of this couch." She smiles at me. "Don't forget it."

"Yes, Stepmother."

Chapter 2

Oh, I hate her.

Hate.

Hate.

Hate.

Actually, I hate everything about my life. Even this street I'm walking on to get to the wretched cloth merchant. It's so quaint and cutesy you would throw up if you saw it. Rows of charming houses, all with pointed roofs, painted shutters, and window boxes full of flowers. Tacky flowers like poppies and geraniums. No sense of style whatsoever.

Hmm.... I straighten the dull gray skirt of my dress as a smile pricks my lips. The royal palace is probably just as cutesy. But that will change when I am queen. Frigid elegance is what I go for. Black marble floors. Silver chandeliers. A throne made of... crystal. Yes, I would like that. A solid crystal throne where I'll sit and wield terror to the people of this paltry kingdom. You're not a true queen unless they're all afraid of you.

"Good day, my lord." I smile suggestively at Lord Burton strolling past, his wife on his arm. He nods uneasily. The wife's eyes are like daggers, first on me, then on him. Jealous, of course, they all are.

I'm not ashamed to say that I'm beautiful. Why should I be modest about it? It took years of stowing up white magic to perfect my appearance. I had to scrub floors for a year to get my hair this golden. Scrape out fireplaces for two winters to straighten the slope of my nose. Mend mountains of stockings and petticoats to shrink the size of my feet. Here, perhaps, I was overly enthusiastic. My feet are really *too* small now, almost like a child's. But I don't mind. Something else for women to envy.

Which brings me back to Stepmother....

I said she treats me like a servant. That's true, of course, but I have to admit it's largely my own doing. Once I discovered that acts of servitude gained me more gooey globs of white magic, I began offering to do chores for my stepmother and stepsisters. The more cheerfully I performed the task, the more white magic I earned. And when Stepmother saw me happily shouldering the work she once paid servants to do, well, why not? She let the servants go and cast it all on me. My chores mounted, my beauty blossomed, but hate curled like briars around my heart.

Because Stepmother changed. I don't see why sweeping stairs and washing linen should suddenly make me inferior, but that is how she acted. And her dimwitted daughters followed suit. Faster than a baby bird plummets from a nest, I became an object of mockery and contempt. The work was no longer requested but commanded. They even seized my bedroom, claiming it would make an "excellent library" and banished me to the empty end of the attic. It's not even a proper room. Just the side where their junk isn't piled.

I reach the cloth merchant, a quaint little shop squished in between the milliner's and the cobbler's. All the shops have red painted doors, big square windows with little square panes, and happy signs. I get in the door and that's as far as I can go.

Ugh. Stepmother was right as raisins. The shop is wall-to-wall women. Bumping, churning, grabbing, yelling, haggling. The floor is lost beneath their skirts, swishing and sliding around each other. One glance at the heavily-shelved wall tells me the red cloth is already gone. No matter. My stepsister Lunilla will be mad but she's always mad. I call her "Loony" to myself.

I inch along the back wall behind the crush of customers, hoping no one treads on my tiny feet. I suck in my stomach and slip around the cumbersome rump of Lady Odelia who can't decide whether to buy pink silk or blue velvet. Puh! As if she's got a chance for the prince in either.

My shoulder bumps the far wall of shelves and here I find some breathing space. No one is interested in the bolts of black and somber gray. My eyes rove over the fabrics as I patiently wait my turn (patient waiting gains more white magic). And that's when I see it: a roll of satin, dark as midnight but luminous as a black pearl. The room behind me fades into mist. I see myself entering the royal ballroom in a gown made of this shimmering darkness, my golden hair glittering above it, the only woman in the whole room wearing black.

Something striking, Stepmother had said.

How could the prince fail to notice?

I curl my fingers around the heavy roll and ease it into my arms like a baby. Somehow, someway, I am going to that ball.

Chapter 3

I guess I should tell you about the white magic.

It's in my room (or my half of the attic). I keep it in a cupboard near my bed, locked. I wear the key on a string around my neck. It's as precious to me as my eyeballs.

Three bolts of cloth lie on my bed. My gorgeous black, garish purple for Loony, and a gentle blue for Moody, my other stepsister. Her real name is Melodie but trust me, there's nothing harmonious about her. Her personality is one flat note, the lowest groan on a pipe organ.

I'm checking my eyes in the small, square mirror that hangs on my wall. They're good. Naturally a nice, pale blue. But this ball, this prince will call for the exceptional. I need eyes like jewels. Like sapphires.

My stupid steps are all out, having their big, knobby feet fitted for new shoes. Lots of luck. Now's a good time to use the white magic.

I lift the string over my head. I click the key into the lock and turn. Behind the wooden door, alone in the cupboard, sits a crystal decanter, much like what my father once used to keep brandy. It's round and beautiful with tiny flashing facets. The decanter holds two inches of white liquid, thick as cream, but giving off a rainbow sheen. I don't know what substance the white magic is made of, but I think of it as melted pearls.

Slowly, reverently, I lower the decanter to my dressing table. I open the top drawer and dig out the silver spoon I use only for white magic. It probably wouldn't make a difference what kind of spoon I use. But to me, details count.

Two inches of liquid. Nineteen months since I last used some magic and the bottle wasn't empty then. That's how hard it is to earn. Washing every window in the house yields, maybe, half a teaspoon. But it's worth it, every bit.

I remove the crystal stopper. Drip by drip, I fill the spoon. I stand before the small mirror to admire the girl within, her immaculate skin, sensuous lips, petal-pink cheeks, delicate chin. All the work of white magic. But thus far I've never touched my eyes.

"Beautiful eyes," I say to the spoon. "Brighter. Bluer. And long lashes."

I swallow the spoonful. It's smooth and sweet, like almond milk and honey cake and a hint of something tropical, like coconut. I close my eyes as the magic becomes sparkles of light that swarm into my irises. It doesn't hurt. Just feels a bit warm and tickly.

I open my eyes. Hmm. A bit bluer, a bit brighter. But not enough. I sigh and tip out another spoonful. I always want to use as little as possible.

"Brighter, bluer, long lashes." And swallow.

I wait for the sparkles to stop their dance beneath my eyelids. Amazing! My eyes are blue as peacock feathers. Bright as stained glass windows with a late sun behind them. But then I notice my lashes, still short.

I curse savagely. Another spoonful. Each one has cost me weeks of chores and cheerfulness. Hundreds of mended stockings. Scrubbing the floor and smiling when Loony steps on my fingers on purpose. Apologizing when Stepmother wonders aloud why the illness took my father and not me - *him* she needed. And I don't know how much magic I'll need to get myself to this ball. Probably all of it.

I swallow. And it's worth it. My lashes are lush, dark brown, curling beautifully around my new eyes. Goddess eyes. Temptress eyes. Eyes that no man can resist.

"Mirror, mirror, on the wall," I whisper. "Who is the fairest one of all?"

The beauty in the mirror grins. Her teeth are white and perfect.

Chapter 4

"CinderelLAH!"

"Yes, Loon – Lunilla?"

"*This* is the dress I want." She points to a page in an illustrated book of fashions and my head wants to explode. Outrageously puffed sleeves and a wide skirt with so many ruffles it'll take ten miles of fabric. Ruffles are torture to sew. Pinch and stitch, pinch and stitch, over and over and over, until you feel trapped and panicky, sentenced to sew for eternity. And I still have to make Moody's dress. And then my own. In two and a half days.

I'm going to die.

I look at Loony. She's a big girl, big all over – chest, hands, nose, teeth – with wild hair, orange as carrots. She likes to wear cherry red and other blazing hues that clash against her hair. Which is why I bought garish purple for her gown. It looked like something she'd wear.

And I was right. Both Loony and Moody liked their fabrics. I know because they said nothing. When they *don't* like what I do, they snarl and yap like nasty little lapdogs. But when I do something right, I get silence. A trick they learned from their mother.

"Don't you think a dressmaker could do it better?" I ask, trying not to sound desperate.

"Undoubtedly. But you're cheaper, at least that's what Mother says. And it better be good and not fall apart while I'm dancing!"

That's a fun image. Loony losing her dress while dancing with the prince. If it weren't for that darn white magic I could arrange it.

I sigh. "What about you, Melodie? Which dress?"

Moody sits on the white couch, looking eternally bored. She resembles Stepmother, brown-haired and blah-faced. She smiles, on average, about once a year.

Moody shrugs her thin shoulders. "Don't care. Don't really want to go." Her voice is as flat as her hair.

"Why don't you stay home?" I say hopefully. If I can be spared one ball gown, so much the better.

"Mother won't let me."

"Of *course* not, don't you get it? This is a chance to be *queen*," Loony says.

"He's too old," Moody drones. Her hand dangles off the arm of the couch, swaying lazily.

"No he's not, he's thirty!" Loony fluffs down on the couch beside her sister. I remember making the corn-yellow dress she's wearing and that took a week. Somebody save me.

"That's ten years older than you," Moody says. "Twelve years older than me and Cindy. It's creepy."

I don't think it's creepy. Quite honestly, I've always had a thing for older men. The lords and dukes and barons of this town, they all like me. They like me very well. Especially when their wives are away. But I soon discovered that such behavior lost me large quantities of white magic, so the men had to go. But they remember and I remember. Like Lord Burton who I passed on the street today, shrinking when I smiled at him. Silly brute, it was only one night.

"I'm just glad he's getting married again," Loony says. "I thought he'd never get over the first wife."

"But there's the daughter," Moody says. "A rotten little apple, I hear. Sorry, but I don't want to be her mother."

"Stepmother," I correct her. I forgot about the daughter. How old would she be now, seven or eight? I don't even know her name.

Our prince, you see, was married before. He had a sweet, smiling wife with shiny black hair and I hated her. And then she did the nicest thing anyone has ever done for me: she dropped dead. Clunk, just like that. No one seems to know what caused it. But it didn't matter because the prince – and my chance to be queen – became available again.

And you never know. The daughter might be just as nice and follow her mother's example. After all, children can have accidents too.

Chapter 5

Sewing hell.

That's where I am.

It's late, my neck is stiff, my fingers cramped. I've got all the pieces cut for Loony's purple monstrosity. Now I'm stitching them together. I need to finish the entire gown tonight. Spend tomorrow making Moody's. Then on the next day, the day of the ball, I can make mine.

But it's not enough time.

I yawn, sucking in the whole night. So, so tired. My stupid steps went to bed hours ago. I wonder if the white magic could perk me up a little. I never tried it for that and don't want to. I will need every drop for the ball.

Our prince's name is Edgar. The name may not be beautiful but oh my, *he* sure is. Blonde like me. A confident grin. I've caught glimpses of him when his carriage rolls through town, just a flash of face in the window. I wonder if his eyes are blue, or green. I wonder if his voice is soft. I wonder if his smile can make me feel snug and safe, like my father's did.

Papa....

I lower my hands, lost under mounds of purple. I'm sitting on a chair beside my bed and now I droop sideways, resting my cheek on the faded quilt. I close my eyes and think about Papa. It smooths the wrinkles in my heart.

Papa. The only person I have to love. You realize I spend a lot of time hating: Stepmother, Loony and Moody, the men who amused themselves with me, the women of this town who stopped speaking to me when I descended from count's daughter to lowly servant. But I can never hate Papa. Dead or alive, everyone needs someone to love, someone to feel with your heart when you close your eyes at night. It's the only thing that keeps me from feeling completely alone.

Papa. When I was a child, he would curl me into his arms, let me tuck my face in his neck. I remember the scratch of his beard on my cheek. We took all of our meal's together, sitting at the table's corner where we could talk companionably, and he'd say, "Tell me what's in your Cinderella head tonight." On days when business tied up his time, he would squeeze my elbow as he hurried past me, a reminder that I was loved even when he couldn't say it.

Papa. The only mistake he ever made was marrying That Woman. But even that I cannot hate him for. He did it for me, to replace the mother I lost at birth and give me sisters to play with. It wasn't a bad idea. They seemed nice at first; I was happy. I tried to ignore the resentment I saw in Stepmother's face when my father kissed my forehead or rustled my hair with his fingers. For his sake, she restrained her contempt, so I never really knew how much she hated me.

And then he died.

My cheek is still on the bed. I feel myself sinking, my thoughts disconnecting. I swim down through layers of sadness and longing, each one darker and deeper. One final thought floats to the surface.

Papa, if you hadn't left me, I'd never have gone bad.

Chapter 6

"CinderelLAH!"

"WHAT?" I shout and my eyes jump nervously to the cupboard. I hope I didn't lose magic over that.

Loony's voice bounds up the attic stairs and bashes into the walls. "Mother wants you right now. So hurry up!" She makes it sound like I'm in trouble.

I heave the half-finished gown onto my bed. Right now I'm in ruffle purgatory. *Maybe* the dress will be finished by nightfall. But today was supposed to be for Moody's dress. I shouldn't have fallen asleep.

Before running downstairs, I check to make sure my rats have water in their bowl. They live in the attic with me, two handsome white rats I call Toil and Trouble. They were once gray. But when

I first received the white magic, I wanted to test it before using it on myself. So I fed it to my rats and their coats turned white and silky. What's more, they gained intelligence and seem to understand when I speak to them. I told them never to leave the attic or my stepsisters will kill them. They listened.

They're the only friends I have.

Stepmother is in her bedroom. Though fully dressed in a stiff burgundy gown, she's lying on the canopied bed, her brow crouching over closed eyes. She slits them open when I enter.

"Are the dresses done?" she asks.

Is she demented? It's been *one* day!

"Not yet, Stepmother," I say gently. "But I'm working hard."

Stepmother sighs and shuts her eyes again. Yes I know, I'm so inadequate.

"My head...." She groans. "I need you to run to the pharmacist for a powder."

"Can Melodie do it? It's a long walk and I need every minute to finish those dresses."

Stepmother merely looks at me. She can say so much with just her eyes. No, Cinderella. Such an errand is beneath my precious daughter. And I take such pleasure in tormenting you.

"Never mind. I'm sorry." I leave the room.

But I have to admit, the long walk is refreshing after hours of sitting in the shady attic. A church bell tolls three o'clock. Sparrows land on the street to pick at crumbs. Carriages roll past me, wheels gobbling over the cobblestones. A nice-looking man smiles at me, someone I've never spoken to.

Phooey....

I hurry, ignoring the burn in my calves. I've got to get back to the dresses. When I return, Stepmother isn't in her room. I listen but hear only Loony and Moody's voices downstairs, gabbling about hairstyles. Well, I'm not scavenging the house for Stepmother. Let her find me herself if she wants her stupid powder.

As I open the door to the attic stairs, I catch the tail end of sound that ceased the moment I opened the door. But I heard it. Little bumps of wood, like a drawer being jiggled.

Or a locked cupboard door.

I fly up the stairs.

Chapter 7

Stepmother stands at my bed, unfolding a bright quilt. My old one is slung on her arm. "Hello, my darling." She smiles at me. "I noticed your cover has grown thin so I brought you a new one. The nights are becoming chilly."

Nice alibi. "Thank you, Stepmother," I say while scanning the room. My rats must have taken refuge behind the trunks and broken tables at the other end of the attic. Good boys.

I keep my eyes on Stepmother because I don't want her to catch me looking at the cupboard. She saunters toward me with a carefully poised smile. "I think you'll be more comfortable now."

"That's very nice of you, considering the awful headache you have." I say it kindly but hope she gets my meaning. I'm not fooled.

She regards me steadily. "Yes, it lifted just after you left. I notice that's often the case. But I'd still like the powder to save for next time."

I hand her the parcel. She hooks her long fingers over it, still watching my face.

"What happened to your eyes?" she asks softly. "They look different today."

I play dumb. "Different?"

"Yes, more... blue."

"Maybe it's the light-"

"It's not the light." Her voice becomes strained, like thin ice under a boot. "And your hair.... Every year it seems to gets lighter. Your father was not so blonde."

Ah. So she noticed. I was never sure. The changes I made to my appearance were gradual, since white magic always took ages to save. Loony and Moody, I know, never noticed, too dense and selfish to see past their own freckles. But at times I have caught Stepmother looking at me, a question folding a line in her brow.

I shrug. "Maybe the sun did it. All those long walks you love to send me on."

Stepmother's eyes narrow and her tone takes a sharper turn. "What's in the cupboard, Cinderella?"

"What cupboard?"

"Do not play games with me. The one you keep locked at all times."

"Oh that?" My mind dives for a quick answer. "Nothing. That cupboard has been locked for ages. I lost the key years ago."

"You mean the key you wear on a string beneath your dress?"

I want to curse. There are times when the key slips out and dangles, like when I'm scrubbing floors or bending to light fires. The old hawk's eyes are sharp.

I can't think of an answer. Her lips curl up in the barest smile. "Open the cupboard."

I meet her frosty gray eyes. "No."

This surprises her. She is used to docility from me. "What?"

"It's my cupboard."

"It's my house."

"No!" My hands start to shake. I want so badly to strike her. "It's *my* house. Mine and my father's. You are the interlopers!"

Stepmother looks stung, offended but not hurt. I can't hurt her because she doesn't love me. Only the people we care about can hurt us.

"Stupid child. You understand nothing!" She swishes past me to descend the attic stairs.

"Get out of my room," I say to her back. "And leave me alone so I can finish making these hideous dresses for your foul... hideous... *DAUGHTERS!*" I screech the last words just as Stepmother closes the door.

Chapter 8

I lunge at the cupboard and open it. The crystal decanter stands tranquil and sedate, but inside the bottle, the surface of the white liquid glitters. I spit a hard curse. The liquid glitters only when I gain magic or lose magic. And my tantrum just now certainly couldn't qualify as good behavior. I lift the decanter to eye level. It still looks like two inches but I know I lost some. Probably a few spoonsful.

I growl and lock the bottle in the cupboard. No more tantrums. Finish the dumb dresses, make your own, go to the ball, win the prince's heart, move out of this house, become queen, find a nice cliff to drop Stepmother off of. That's all.

Sigh....

I sew until the sun is long forgotten, until my candles sputter down to stubs. Until my head flops around like a homespun doll's, until the night is silent as a cave. Even my rats are asleep.

Done with Loony's gown. Cutting the pieces for Moody's. Tomorrow is the ball. What time will it be? Seven? Eight? I can't remember. The stitches are blurred and I can't bring them into focus. I prick my finger with the needle again and suck a drop of blood into my mouth. It makes me thirsty.

My body slides out of the chair. Fine, I'll take some magic. But just one spoonful. I have to keep sewing.

Four tries before I manage to aim the key at the keyhole. I droop against the wall and fill the silver spoon. "Awake," is all I can say. I'm almost too tired to swallow it.

The warm sparkles sink into my body, then rise up through my head. And I'm awake. Not bouncy or cheerful, but I can think now. And sit straight. I pick the pieces of Moody's gown off the floor and flop into the chair again. Get it done. Get it done. Get it done.

Chapter 9

Moody stands on a footstool in her bedroom while I pin up the hem. It's nearly eleven o'clock on the morning before the ball. I almost don't care. The white magic has worn off and I'm so desperately tired I could sleep a hundred years.

"Why is her dress so plain?" Stepmother asks. She's standing behind me, stern as a palace guard.

I chose a simple design for Moody's gown because that's what she likes. But it's nice. Periwinkle blue with a smooth skirt, a swirling pattern of silver beads sewn across the bodice. It's tasteful, unlike Loony's riotous ruffles.

"It's fine, Mother." Moody says. "I just want to get this over with."

"Bad attitude!" Loony's sitting on the bed in her petticoat and swinging her big feet. She's smiling. Probably thinks her chances for the prince are better if Moody doesn't care. She might be right. If the prince wants a loud-mouthed tomato for a wife.

Stepmother taps her chin and frowns at Moody's dress. "She needs some pin tucks in the skirt to give it more lift. And put some padding into the bodice to fill out her bosom-"

"Motherrr!" Moody whines.

"What? It's no secret you're flat as a floor." Loony cackles while Moody throws a murderous look. "At least *my* chest doesn't fall on my lap when I sit down."

Loony frowns. "Are you calling me fat?"

"Well, if the shoe fits-"

"Come, come, girls," Stepmother says. I'm glad she stopped them. I've seen my stepsisters fight before and it's like cats, all clawing and hissing. I don't care if they go to the ball with red scratches on their faces but they could ruin Moody's gown.

"You can take it off now," I say to Moody. "I'll make the changes quickly." I also have adjustments to make for Loony's gown, the waist and shoulders proved too tight. Stepmother blamed my measurements rather than face the fact that her daughter gained another pound in two days.

"What will *you* do while we're dancing with the prince, Cindy?" Loony smirks at me. I gather Moody's dress into my arms. "Sleep."

Loony laughs. "Well, that's all you're good at."

"Oh, that reminds me, I gave Cook the night off," Stepmother says. Cook is the only servant she kept besides me and thank goodness for that. I don't know how to toast bread. "She wants to help her niece prepare for the ball and of course I understood. She intended to harvest the pumpkins today and place them in the cellar before the nights get too cold. I told her you would take care of it."

So after long days of sewing with practically no sleep, Stepmother wants me to spend the evening hauling heavy pumpkins indoors. There are no words for how much I hate her.

"And before you make those adjustments, Cinderella," Stepmother goes on, enjoying herself, "I need you to run down to the cobbler's and pick up my daughters' dancing slippers. They should be done by now."

Another long walk. Then the dress alterations. And before the ball tonight, I *have* to get a little sleep. My own gown is still a bundle of cloth, a black mummy on my bed. For the first time, I wonder if I'll make it to this ball at all.

Chapter 10

They look nice, Loony and Moody. At least as nice as it's possible for them to look. Their hair is up, adorned with flowers. The gowns fit, the colors suit, even Loony's loud purple. She looks pleased with herself, a horse groomed for a parade. And I have to admit there is grandeur about her. Moody looks sulky but that's normal for her. I pinned her flat, dark hair into a tight roll above her neck and if she slouched a little less, she could be graceful.

Oh well. Not my concern.

Stepmother wears dove grey silk and a shawl of black lace. I can see she approves of her daughters but won't voice her admiration so long as I'm present. I don't deserve even an indirect compliment.

The hired coach arrives. My stupid steps rustle out of the house, Stepmother murmuring a reminder about the pumpkins. I slump against the doorframe and watch the coach drive out to the gate. Night is spilling into the sky, staining the clouds purple.

Six-thirty. The ball will start at seven. And my dress is not made.

I climb the stairs to the attic with bones like iron. I haven't slept in over twenty-four hours. If I use the white magic, I won't have enough for the ball. But I guess I'm not going to the ball.

I move the bolt of black cloth off my bed and onto the chair. The thought of sewing one more stitch makes me want to hurl myself out the window. I can't. Could the white magic make a dress for me? I'm not sure. And I still need shoes, a coach and horses, a driver, and the other enhancements I planned. Two inches of liquid. No, it's not enough.

I lie on the bed and shut my eyes. It's no use. I'll never be anything but an unwanted orphan. I just wanted to be special. Admired and honored and loved. It doesn't matter. If I don't sleep now I will die.

Mmm.... How wonderful that sounds.

Chapter II

I snap awake. The attic is nothing but dark shapes and shadows. I was dreaming about Papa. He was shaking my shoulder and laughing. "Get up, Cinder-lazy, it's time to go!" His smile warmed me through, like broth on a winter evening.

I roll out of bed and check the window. The stars are out thick but I spot a stray carriage turning up a nearby street and two old women chatting on their doorstep. It can't be too late.

I load my arms with the bundled cloth, the decanter of white magic, the silver spoon, and a candle to see my way. I hurry down the attic stairs, smiling because I just saw my father. As real and touchable as my own skin. He believes in me. He wants me to go.

"I can do this, Papa," I say. "I know I can."

I check the time on a standing clock in the hall. Just after nine. All right, so I'll be atrociously late. But I'm going! If Papa thinks I can, I'll have enough white magic to do it. Right?

I bustle out the door that leads to the courtyard behind the house. I'm so excited I feel like singing. Before Papa woke me, I was having an odd dream about riding to the ball inside a pumpkin which my rats pulled behind them like a coach. Weird, of course, but it gave me a wild idea.

Let's see if this white magic is worth its mettle!

The courtyard is long and narrow, one end open to the street behind us. The pumpkin patch lies to the right, behind a short iron fence. A tangle of vines and curling leaves crawling around the bright orange pumpkins. I pick the largest I can find and carry it to the yard, brushing off the dirt before I set it down on the cobblestones.

Transportation comes first. It won't matter how fabulous I look if I can't go anywhere. The palace is six miles away, too far to walk on foot. And I'm sure every rentable coach has been taken by now.

A pumpkin it is.

I crouch beside the pumpkin and clink the top off the decanter. I pour out a spoonful of white magic and tip the spoon over the pumpkin. It pools into the depression created by the stalk. "A magnificent carriage," I say. And wait.

Nothing.

I blow the air out of my cheeks. "Darn it." I pour another spoonful. "A magnificent carriage!" I say louder. The white liquid rises a bit higher in the hollow.

Still nothing.

Hmm.... I'm not discouraged yet. I trust the white magic, it has never failed me. Maybe I should leave off the word 'magnificent'.

"All right. Just a carriage." I add a third spoonful and the white liquid runs down the grooves of the pumpkin. It begins to sparkle....

I jump back in joyous anticipation. The pumpkin glitters, swells, turns white as a pearl – and stops.

I start to laugh. "What?" I've got a big, white pumpkin, half my height, with a little door in the center. But it's working. It's working!

Three more spoonsful – "A magnificent carriage!" - and the pumpkin blossoms into the most beautiful white coach I have ever seen, complete with gold embellishments, cushioned benches, and a high seat in front for a driver. It's amazing. It fills the whole courtyard and almost seems to glow. I just stand there gaping at it before I remember that time is precious.

Horses, that's next. I dash back to my attic and scoop up Toil and Trouble. As I'm rushing down again, I explain what I plan to do and promise to change them back as soon as I can. I can't say they look thrilled about it but they don't try to wriggle away from me.

In the courtyard, I lower the spoonful of magic to their tiny mouths. They sniff at it, whiskers quivering, before reluctantly lapping it up. When one spoon doesn't work, I feed them a second and then a third and then a fourth. The rats twinkle and before my eyes grow into gorgeous white stallions. Even with bridles! They paw the ground awkwardly, as if testing their long legs and hooves. I pat Trouble's cheek. "Thank you, sweetie."

I check the crystal decanter. Oh dear. A whole inch of white magic is gone. Only one inch left. I hope it will be enough.

A driver.... That's going to be hard. For one thing, I don't have another animal. And the thought of creating a human from an animal sounds absolutely creepy... and somehow forbidden.

Let me think on that. In the meantime, I'll use a little magic on myself. I need the enhancements I planned. Qualities I hope will make me irresistible to the prince.

I pour myself a spoonful. "Charming," I say and swallow it. I take another spoon for good measure. One never seems to be enough.

Two more spoons for "Graceful." Two more for "Alluring." And finally, I swallow three spoonsful and say, "Whatever the prince desires most."

The vagueness of this worries me. I'm not sure if the white magic is capable of knowing what I don't. But the sparkles buzz warm in my chest which means it must be working.

Not much left in the bottle now. Maybe two spoonsful? That won't be enough for a coachman. Maybe I can grab a fellow off the street and pay him from my meager wages.

It better be enough for my dress.

Feeling a bit nervous, I stand the roll of cloth against a wheel of the carriage. No need for the silver spoon this time. I pour the last of the magic straight onto the fabric and say, "A beautiful, black ball gown."

I wait.

Not a single sparkle.

And the white magic is gone.

I begin to pace quickly. Drat! Darn it! Papa made me too sure I would have enough magic. I should have asked for a plain carriage or left off 'graceful' as one of my enhancements. I should have held back that tantrum yesterday which cost me the last few spoons that I need. All of that would be better than the option facing me.

There's only one way I'll get to this ball now. Only one person, one creature who can help me. I'm going to have to call on *her*. The crazy woman.

I call her Godnutter.

Chapter 12

I pace a little longer, trying to think of something else. Oh Papa, please, anything but her! But I know it's no use. She's better than nothing – sort of – and I'm desperate. So here goes.

"Fairy Godmother, come to my aid, help me to fix this mess that I've made." Yes, that's really what she told me to say.

I stare at the starry sky and wait.

"Hello, brat."

I nearly jump out of my shoes. I whirl around with my hand on my chest. "Crackers, Godnutter, can't you make a little noise? Stir the wind before you come?"

She's right behind me, large and solid. Looking, as usual, like she just rolled out of bed. Her gray hair is piled in a lopsided bun with sprays that stick out like weeds. She wears a green dress, slightly crumpled, and her transparent wings point out behind her. And, like always, she's smoking.

Godnutter laughs, shooting smoke from her mouth. "Good gravy, look at you! What have you done to yourself?"

"What?"

"You look like a freaky doll! We should set you up in a shop window where you can bat those false eyelashes." She pokes the clay pipe back in her mouth and turns her eyes to the enormous carriage. "Ooh, look at that!"

"They're not false, it's white magic! The white magic *you* gave me to better myself!"

Godnutter rolls her eyes and sucks the long, curling tip of her pipe. "It was supposed to make you a better person. You've abused it, muffin."

"How? You said I couldn't hurt anyone with it and I haven't."

"Not directly, no. But you've made yourself so freakishly beautiful that most women feel depressed when they look at you."

I smile. "That's good."

"You're too obsessed with your appearance."

"What are you, my mother?"

"No, but unlike you, I knew her. And she would not be proud of you."

I scowl and fold my arms. "Would she be proud of *you?*" That gets her. She turns away from me and puffs a cloud of wounded pride.

Godnutter is my mother's sister. I never knew she existed until my father died when I was twelve. After the burial service, I stood weeping over my father's grave. Stepmother had not shed a tear, had rebuked me for being 'emotional' in public. But when they all left, I found a minute to mourn my father in solitude. Suddenly Godnutter was beside me, pipe and all, and I freaked out.

She explained who she was and told me a sad story. She had once been a human lady, married to a nice man. But they had a terrible quarrel and Godnutter swung a pewter candlestick at his head. He died. And Godnutter, overcome with guilt, had thrown herself off the roof of her house. But it wasn't high enough. She lay on the pavement, broken and bleeding, waiting to die, when the fairies came.

I have never seen fairies. I'm told they keep to themselves and help us humans in quiet, invisible ways. But the fairies took pity on Godnutter. They said they could not save her human life, but if she became one of them, a fairy, she could help other unfortunate people and make amends for her terrible deed. Godnutter agreed. But, as she liked to tell me, she didn't know then they would assign her to *me.*

I remember her offering the crystal decanter. "What is it?" I asked. "Magic," she whispered. "The fairies tell me you have darkness inside you. Just a kernel, a seedling. But we think that woman, your stepmother, is going to make it grow. You will be tempted to return cruelty for cruelty. And I don't want you turning out bad, as I did."

"What do I do with this?" I took the decanter, pleased with its glittering beauty.

"Every time you choose to be good, you'll receive a little white magic in the bottle. The magic can make your life better in small ways. It can turn a crust of bread into cake. It can heal your body of aches and ills. It can make your heart happy when it should be sad. It can do almost anything you want it to, so long as you do not harm another person."

"Sure," I said at the time, because why would I ever want to hurt anyone? "Thank you." I hoped she would leave me then. I liked the gift but Godnutter was scary.

"Be good, Cinderella, and all will end happily." Then she freaked me out again by fading into air.

And thus the white magic took over my life.

Chapter 13

The first thing I did was turn my rats white. Then I fixed my crooked teeth. Then, just for kicks, I turned a pair of my shoes into gold. But Loony got jealous and stole them away and Stepmother didn't make her give them back. I started shrinking my feet so my shoes wouldn't fit her.

Then one day, I heard Stepmother remark to a neighbor that I was "somewhat pretty but nothing special." And that burnt a hole right through my heart. Papa had always called me beautiful, his little queen. I decided I would make myself so stunning, I really *could* be queen. The fairest in the land. The idea rooted into my heart, sprouted and flourished and bloomed. I didn't know *how* I would meet and marry the prince, but I waited for an opportunity.

And now it's here.

Godnutter crosses the yard and dumps the ashes of her pipe into the pumpkin patch. "All right, brat, why am I here? What do you want?"

"I want to go to the ball."

"What ball?"

"Oh gracious, what goes on in fairyland? The prince's ball!"

Godnutter digs in the pocket of her dress and pulls out a little pouch that holds the stuff she smokes. "Hmm, sounds dreary. Why don't you stay home and play cards? We could have a nice game of cribbage."

"Do fairies play cards?"

"All the time, and cheat like thieves."

"Um, no thanks. I really want to go to the ball."

"Why?"

"Well, the prince is looking for a new bride and I thought it would be... nice... if he chose me. It could happen. And it would get me away from Stepmother and Loony and Moody."

"Who?"

"Lunilla and Melodie."

"That's what you call them? Ha!" Godnutter cackles, a loud, smoky rattle. She snaps her fingers over the pipe and it lights again. "So have you met this prince?" she mumbles, mouth around the pipe.

"No, not yet."

"But you want to marry him. Ooh, real smart."

I sigh heavily. Can't I have one nice relative? Just one? Is that too much to ask? "I want to be queen, that's all. I don't care about the prince."

Godnutter simply puffs and stares.

"So will you help me?"

"Hmm...." Godnutter blows out a cloud of smoke and watches it sift into the air. "No."

I clench my teeth. The white magic is gone, I don't *have* to be patient. But if I blow up she might disappear and then I'm stuck.

I try a softer tone. "I think Papa wants me to go. He came to me in a dream tonight."

"A dream is a wish your heart makes. It wasn't really him."

"Why won't you help me!" I whine. "You're my fairy godmother, that's what you're for!"

"I'm not your genie, honeybun. I'm here to look out for you. You know, fairies can't see the future. Only shadows and suggestions. And something tells me this ball is bad news."

"I still want to go."

"Then give me a reason."

"What?"

"Give me a *reason* to let you go."

I think about this. A reason. Something I can offer in exchange, like a bargain or deal. What does she want from me? What would be hard for me to give up?

My eyes fall to the crystal decanter standing on the flagstones and I curse inwardly.

"If you let me go to this ball," I say slowly, "and *if* I fail to win the prince's hand, I will give you back the white magic. And I'll be *good*. Just for goodness' sake."

Godnutter lifts her frizzled eyebrows. "And," she says, "*if* you fail, I will reverse the changes the white magic has wrought. You'll be ordinary Cinderella again."

Ordinary Cinderella. The crooked teeth. The slopey nose. The straw-colored hair. And who knows how big my feet will be? My stomach turns inside out just thinking about it.

"That or nothing, dumpling," Godnutter says.

I grit my teeth - "Deal." - then turn and drop my face in my hands. Oh Papa, what have I done?

Godnutter slaps my bottom and laughs. "Let's get you to this ball, brat!"

Chapter 14

Godnutter walks the length of the carriage, inspecting it. "Well, this looks fancy. The horses too. Must've taken a lot of the stuff, didn't it?"

"Yes," I grumble. You'd think I'd be happy but my good mood is gone. That was a hard bargain. Now I *have* to win the prince.

"No coachman though." Godnutter looks up at the empty driver's seat. "Huh. Go get that mouse over there."

"What mouse?"

"The one in those weeds, beyond the yard!" She stands there, looking casually at the house, one arm lifting that blasted pipe to her mouth. And waits for me to find the mouse.

Does she think I'm an owl that can spot a tiny mouse in the dark? Ugh, I almost hate her. But I shuffle around the grass until I finally see it, hiding between some rocks. He must be sleepy or something because I have no trouble catching him. I carry him, wriggling and squeaking, back to Godnutter.

"Now put him down," she says, bossy-like.

I set him down and he shoots off like lightning. Godnutter calmly removes the pipe from her mouth and waves the stem in circular motions. A stream of white sparkles flies from the tip to the mouse, and suddenly he springs up, tall and human and liveried. A driver.

Godnutter's pipe is a magic wand. I did not see that coming.

The driver stands before us, silent and trembling. His quiet, dark eyes are the scariest things I've ever seen. To anyone else I guess he'll look normal, even kind of handsome. But all I can think is, mouse. Mouse, mouse, a human mouse. That's sick.

"Don't be afraid, dear," Godnutter speaks to him gently. "Just climb up to that seat, there's a good boy. You'll know what to do."

The mouse-driver meekly obeys. I decide not to look at him anymore. I run to the wheel where my black cloth is standing and bring it back to

Godnutter. "I need a ball gown!" I say breathily. I'm getting excited now, this is the best part.

Godnutter looks at the fabric, then at my face. "Black," she says flatly.

"Yes, please."

"A *black* dress."

"Will you just do it?"

Godnutter exhales and her breath is pungent and stale. "Hold it over yourself."

I let the fabric unroll, holding it from my shoulders like a sheet. Godnutter shakes her head, mutters "black" to herself, and then swivels the pipe stem around, scattering ashes out of the bowl.

A bright river of sparkles strikes the cloth, then swirls around me, and for a moment I'm lost in a hailstorm of light. My eyes are dazzled and I can't see Godnutter. Something cool and slippery-soft wraps my waist and arms and back. The sparkles dissolve, drifting like snowflakes to the ground. I look down.

And gasp.

It's more exquisite than I imagined. A luminous black ball gown, snug over my torso, then billowing out in a plush skirt. Layers cut over layers, the edges overlapping in long points that look like leaves. The collar dips low on my chest but rises high behind my neck in a spread of gauzy feathers. I look like a dark angel. A beautiful nightmare.

"Oh! Thank you, Fairy Godmother!" I take two steps toward her and my feet *clink, clink* on the cobblestones. I bend over and lift the hem of my skirt. My shoes! They're made of crystal! Beautiful and twinkling, like the bottle of white magic. My pretty feet show through them, lifted up on high, slender heels. Crystal slippers. I'm so happy I could cry.

"Good gravy, can you even walk on those feet?" Godnutter looks horrified. "That's *too* small, honey, you look deformed!"

I'm too ecstatic to let her bother me. "Thank you so much!" I swoop in and kiss her cheek. "This is everything I ever wanted!"

She pats my shoulder. "In that case, I failed you miserably. But never mind, off you go." She snaps open the door of the carriage and I gather my skirt to climb inside. The seat is wonderfully soft. I turn and take hold of the open door, gripping the bottom edge of its window. "Wish me luck!" I grin at Godnutter.

"May it be the evening you deserve. Have fun and watch those feet. And by the way, I want you home at midnight."

The smile drops right off my face. "Uh... what?"

"You heard me. Home at the stroke of twelve and not a second later."

"What time is it *now*? Nearly ten?"

"That gives you two wonderful hours to win the prince's heart. Good luck!"

"Why? Why midnight?"

Godnutter glowers at me. "Let's just say I've noticed your evenings with *men* run a lot later than I approve of. I don't want you misbehaving with this prince. And if you're thinking of disobeying me," she wags the pipe stem at me, "I have set the spell so everything that's been enchanted will turn back to it's true form at midnight. Even the things you put white magic on! You'll have nothing but a pumpkin, two rats, a mouse, and a dowdy dress. So watch the clock or it could get quite embarrassing!"

I slam the door shut. "Drop dead, Godnutter!" I shout as the carriage begins to roll.

"I already did that!" she calls after me, following it with her nasty cackle. I look back and the spot where she stood is now vacant. But her crazy laugh lingers, chasing me into the night.

Chapter 15

The carriage stops before the palace. The driver surprises me by hopping down and holding the door.

"Oh. Thank you." I step down without looking at him. "Um... find a place to park. Then meet me here again at-" I groan "-quarter to midnight." I tried to regain my excitement during the drive. But knowing you have less than two hours to get a marriage proposal from a prince you haven't met or be doomed forever to mediocrity can be something of a downer.

The driver climbs back to his seat and flicks the reins. I'm glad he doesn't speak – he's creepy enough.

Oh my.... I've never been this close to the palace before. It's impressive. Soaring walls of cream-colored stone. Lots of towers, some blunt and bulging, others slender and sky high. One of the central towers displays a massive clock with a dark face and shining gold hands. Twenty past ten. Oh dear....

I'm standing at the bottom of a huge, round staircase with steps that ripple down to me like rings in a pond. At the top, a massive set of double doors stands open, a cave of golden light. The swift, lifting notes of a waltz beckon to me from within.

I pinch my skirt and climb the stairs. No one stops me from walking right in. Two palace guards stand on either side of the doors but they just look at me. Or rather, at my dress. I suppress a smug smile. I knew black would be good.

A bright hallway stretches before me, leading to another pair of open doors. That must be the ballroom. My heart begins to float with the music I hear inside. I can't believe I'm here. I can't believe it.

My whole body quivers as I creep into the ballroom. Ohhh! This must be heaven. Because no man could create a place of such majestic wonder.

I'm at the top of another staircase, looking out over the ballroom. I never knew one room could be so enormous. Hundreds of couples bobbing and swirling, like leaves twirled by the wind. A white marble floor so glossy it reflects the people upside-down in a kind of milky mirror. A vaulted ceiling, impossibly high, and painted all over with clouds and angels and rays of celestial light. Dark windows tall as trees, and chandeliers that dangle teardrops of crystal, dripping rainbows around the room. I do like crystal.

Resting my hand on the golden railing, I descend the staircase gently, not wanting to crack or break my fragile shoes. My dress slips down each step behind me, black over white. I catch several people staring up at me and I wear the expression I planned in the carriage: serene and slightly cold. I want to look mysterious.

My foot has barely touched the floor when I find no less than four men surrounding me. Three young men and one older, all smiling. "Good evening, my lady," says a man in the middle. "Would you care to dance?"

"No, allow me, my lady, I can introduce you-"

"Hey, I saw her first!" a third man cries.

Ugh. The allurement enhancement. I should have been more specific, said it was for the prince only. This means a lot of men are going to give me trouble.

"Excuse me," I say firmly and skirt around them.

I've taken only a few more steps when something grabs my attention more than the grandeur surrounding me. A smell. Faint but distinct, the aroma of roasted chicken.

Oh my goodness. I'm *starving!*

When did I eat last? I remember grabbing a hunk of dry bread before I ran out to fetch my stepsisters' dancing shoes. In the past three days I've had almost as little food as sleep. But now that I remember food exists, I feel like I'll die if I don't get some right now.

But – I look for a clock and don't see one – I don't have time to eat. I have to find the prince.

Still, the smell leads me onward, around the dancers and along the wall, where clumps of hopeful mothers watch from the sidelines. I'll just have a little something. A quick bite. It'll give me a minute to make my plans and then I'll get to work.

I pass a mirror that sprawls across a large section of wall and I turn my head for a quick glance.

And stop cold.

I look dazzling! The black dress blooming out around me, the high, feathery collar behind my neck. And my hair! Piled up on my head, a bit loose and chaotic, rather like Godnutter's. But it works with this dress. And I've got a tiara I didn't even know about. A silver tiara with sharp, flashing points. I look like a queen already. An evil queen, the best kind.

I almost forgive Godnutter for the curfew. Almost.

Toward the back of the ballroom I find a collection of small round tables. Most of them are empty now. A few couples are sitting and talking over thick slices of pie. But I don't want pie. I want chicken.

I'm standing there, not sure what to do, when a little servant girl appears and asks if I'd like to eat something. I tell her chicken, and vegetables, and bread, and wine. Then I find a table and wait, my toes twitching inside my rock-hard shoes. I can't say they're terribly comfortable.

A stout young man looms up to my table. "Sitting alone, fair lady?" He asks with a heavy smile.

"Yes!" I snap and the man backs off. Oh brother. Why are the men here anyway? I guess the ladies needed escorts but the men must know the truth. This is all a colossal headhunt for the prince. His Royal Highness may think he's selecting a bride but it's the other way around. He is the rabbit. And we are the wolves.

I haven't seen the prince yet. Or anyone else I know, the faces gliding past me are strangers. I amuse myself by watching the women, they're all beautiful. Well not all, but a great many. Their gowns are lavish, their hair curled and braided and jeweled. A few of them wear tiaras but none as fancy as mine.

The little servant girl brings me a steaming plate and I'm so hungry I want to tear into it with my fingers. But I force myself to eat decorously. The chicken is wonderful, moist and smoky, unlike the bland cuts of wood Cook serves to us at home.

I'm starting to like this palace.

I don't stop watching for the prince. I peer into the crowd, check the room from side to side. As

I'm turning my head I notice the person sitting at the table next to mine and almost jump.

It's Moody. Sitting alone and looking right at me.

I've got a mouthful of chicken so I can't speak. Moody simply looks at me, mildly curious, then lets her lifeless eyes drift back to the ballroom. I continue to stare at her. That was odd. The way she looked at me.... Almost as if... she didn't recognize me?

Gracious, I don't look *that* different! My face is the same, I just saw it in the mirror. Is she really that dense?

"Hello," I say, just to test it.

She looks back. "Good evening." She says it so politely I *know* she doesn't recognize me. That's so bizarre.

"Are you enjoying the ball?" I ask.

"Not a bit," she says. "You?"

I laugh. "I just got here. Awfully late, I'm afraid."

"You haven't missed much," Moody says dryly. "Eating and dancing, dancing and eating. A long, boring speech from King Stephen. That's all."

"Did you dance with the prince?"

Moody shakes her head. "Don't want to. I've been sitting here alone all night. Wish my sister was here."

"Your sister?" Loony? She has to be here somewhere. Probably swimming around the prince with the rest of the sharks.

"Yes, she stayed at home. My mother wouldn't let her come to the ball."

Is she talking about... me? And referring to me as a sister, not a step. "Why do you want her here?" I have to ask.

Moody shrugs. "She would enjoy this. And if she didn't, at least I'd have someone to talk to. Mother's being stupid. Cindy has a better chance for the prince than anyone. She's pretty. And unlike Lunilla, she's smart."

A hard, frozen section of my heart begins to thaw. Moody likes me. Or at least doesn't hate me. I remember when we played together, that first year before Papa died. We would braid each other's hair before bed. I could even make her laugh sometimes. Then, when Stepmother began to segregate me, Moody turned cold, probably afraid of defying her mother. But sometimes, when I came to make her bed in the morning, she would speak to me, a few flat sentences that I thought meant nothing. But she never got nasty, like Loony did. Maybe in her dull, emotionless way she felt sorry for me. Just didn't know how to show it.

Well. That's something.

Moody lifts a lazy finger. "That's my other sister, Lunilla."

I look up. Two people have spiraled onto the outer edge of dancers. One is Loony, her ruddy face even ruddier with exertion. And she's dancing with-

The prince!

There he is! And he looks fabulous. Dressed in a slim white suit, edged in gold. Lunilla is running her mouth, of course, and he listens with a polite smile. I grab the napkin beside my plate and wipe the grease off my fingers. I've sighted my quarry.

It's time to join the hunt.

Chapter 16

I turn to rise and stop short. A little girl stands a few feet away, watching me. She looks no more than eight years old and wears a fluffy white dress with lots of lace. This, clearly, is the prince's daughter. I've seen no other children here.

She steps closer to me. "Why are you wearing that?" And points to my dress.

I smile. "Do you like it?"

"It's ugly," she says. "Did somebody die?"

"No, I just like black." My tone is colder now. I'm not enchanted with this little girl. For one thing, she's awfully pretty. Her hair is raven black and flows freely to her waist. Her skin is pale and porcelain smooth. She needs no white magic to perfect her appearance, she will naturally grow into a breathtaking beauty. It isn't fair.

The girl points to my head. "Your crown is nice, though. Where did you get it?"

"It's a tiara. I, um, borrowed it from a friend."

"May I wear it for a while?" The girl holds out her hand, expectant.

I hesitate. "Well... perhaps later. I need it until the ball is over."

The girl keeps her hand out and expertly lifts a single eyebrow. "I want it *now*, if you please."

I look straight into her haughty brown eyes. "No."

The girl's hand drifts downward. She's shocked. I guess a princess is used to getting her way. Not with me. I've got this tiara for ninety more minutes, and prince's daughter or not, the little brat can't have it.

I'm hoping she'll leave me now, go off somewhere to sulk. But suddenly she lunges and snatches the tiara right out of my hair! With a high laugh she dashes away, throwing herself straight into the churning crowd of dancers.

I jump up, grinding my teeth. The prince is gone; I lost track of him when his daughter appeared. And now she has *my* tiara. I will get it back if I have to break her little arm.

I barge right into the midst of the dancing couples. It's like trying to walk through a moving forest. I see the girl ahead, sprinting around the wide, swishy skirts. A few people step aside for the princess, but most of them don't notice her and she's getting blocked and slowed, as I am. But she is smaller, quicker, and not wearing breakable shoes. The distance between us grows.

I growl and push harder, not caring who I bump or that I'm drawing hostile stares. I stay focused on the girl, just a flash of white dress among the hordes. She's nearing the top of the ballroom and the long staircase with golden railings. I spy a sudden opening to my left, a clear path between the dancers. I race through, hoping this will catch me up.

I break out of the crowd just before the stairs. The girl bursts out at the same moment, my tiara still clutched in her grubby fingers. She sees me. She makes a frantic dash up the staircase but I leap and grab a fistful of her flying hair, jerking her to a stop. "Give it back, you little freak!" I snarl.

"Yes, sweetheart," says a man's voice. "Please give the lady back her tiara."

I drop my hand and straighten like a puppet yanked on its strings. *The prince.* Standing just below us, his hands clasped casually at his back. He's looking at his daughter, not me. And he's smiling.

The princess is on the fourth step, twisting to look at her father. Her eyes are rebellious. The prince calmly lifts a hand and says, "Give it here, darling."

The girl slaps the tiara into his hand and stomps up the steps, muttering. The prince turns to me with a gentle smile. Surprising, considering he just caught me pulling his daughter's hair and calling her a freak. But all he says is, "Please forgive my daughter, she can be mischievous at times. I believe this is yours?"

"Thank you," I murmur, still flustered. I take the tiara and settle it back into my hair. Remembering my manners, I sink into a deep and graceful curtsy. "Good evening, Your Highness. I am sorry for the disturbance."

"Nothing at all," he says pleasantly. I like the way he looks at me, as if I'm something rare and exotic. This is what I hoped for.

He smiles and offers his arm. "Well. Now that that's over, would you care for a dance?"

I sigh and laugh. "Gladly!"

We stroll onto the dance floor where everyone makes room for the prince and his partner. He slips his hand on my waist, smiles, and we begin.

Oh, it's wonderful. Like dreaming. We glide swiftly and smoothly around the ballroom, perfectly timed to the music and each other. Memories float up of those beautiful years when Papa and I lived alone and he'd push back the dining room table and teach me how to dance, humming the music himself. And look at me now, in the royal palace, dancing with the prince.

I still wish it was you, Papa.

"So. They call me Prince Edgar." The prince grins and it's dazzling. He has strong, handsome features, a good chin, clear blue eyes. His blonde hair is cut short, a bit fluffy on top. We must look great together, my black dress weaving with his white suit. Like day and night, good and evil.

"So happy to finally meet you, Prince Edgar. Do you know this is my first time in the palace?"

"I thought so!" Prince Edgar takes my hand, twirls me on the spot, then clasps my waist again. "I knew I couldn't have seen you before. I would have remembered."

"Well, I don't get out much," I say lightly. I keep my eyes on his, my face lifted, my lips parted just slightly. Come on, white magic, don't fail me now.

"And what do they call *you?*" he asks with a subtle lift of his eyebrows. Boy, he's good. My heart flops around like a fish on dry land.

But I'm hesitant to reveal my name because I'm still worried about the incident with his daughter. The prince brushed that off just a bit too easily. Furthermore, his parents – King Stephen and Queen Shelley – are here tonight, I saw them dancing. If that nasty little princess learns my name, she might go blabbing to the king. And I do *not* want to end my evening in the dungeon. So my name can wait until I've thoroughly hooked the prince's heart.

I offer a coy smile. "You may call me whatever you like, Your Highness."

Prince Edgar laughs. "Are you some kind of dark secret? You look it, in that dress."

"Do you like it?"

"It's perfect. You're like a little crow that's come to haunt me."

"Then call me Crow." I grin at him.

We dance and the minutes slip like sand through my fingers. My charm enhancement does wonders, never did I find speaking so easy. Our conversation flows as seamlessly as our feet, never faltering or missing a step.

Once, and only once, do I spot Stepmother. She's over by the wall with Loony, both of them watching me. My stomach twitches when I catch Stepmother's eye, but her look, though irritated, shows no sign of recognition. I know Stepmother by now. If she knew it was me, she'd be white with rage. She'd find sly ways to humiliate me, like tripping my feet or dropping a spider into my hair. And Loony, well, Loony would probably rip me to shreds in front of everyone.

Godnutter's spell. Has to be. She knew my stupid steps would never leave me alone otherwise. She did it to protect me, to let me enjoy the night. I really should forgive her for imposing the curfew.

But I won't.

The music ends and we sway to a stop. "Hot?" Prince Edgar asks.

I laugh. "Terribly."

"Let's go out for a bit, walk under the stars." He curls an arm around my shoulders. "If you promise not to fly away, of course."

"I think my wings are too tired."

We begin to thread our way out of the ballroom. I do enjoy the looks I'm getting from other ladies. Frustration. Envy. Unconcealed hatred. They will hate me more when I am queen.

I will see to that.

Chapter 17

The night is cool, soft as feathers. I walk with Prince Edgar on a terrace that stretches a long arm out from the castle. The moon hovers like a bright pearl, quiet and graceful. It's a lovely night – a finer night I know I'll never see. Edgar is delightful and we talk long and easily, rambling about our childhoods, places we've visited, the best kind of riding horse, how we both don't like pork much, whether stars are white or gold, even touching on fashion. I feel as if I found the friend I lost when Papa died. With Edgar, I could even be good.

The terrace is key-shaped, ending in a wide circle. It surrounds a lonely tower, a pale finger of stone cutting high into the night. To our right, a staircase drops from the terrace to the gardens where I see sculpted shrubbery and paths that curl around flower beds. I'm guessing we'll go down to the gardens, but Edgar invites me to sit with him on an iron bench by the wall.

"Enjoying yourself?" He takes my hand and my heart crashes inside me. I can't stop smiling. "This is the most wonderful night of my life!" And I mean it.

Edgar releases my hand and leans back, folding his arms. "Glad to hear it. Now tell me, what would being queen do for you?"

Oh my goodness. Oh my *goodness!* Is this really happening? I want to squeal like a little girl, bounce in my seat. I can't believe I'm going to win.

"It would... be wonderful!" I cry. "A dream come true!"

"And why did you dream of being queen? Specifically?" His smile is different now. Careful. Detached.

"What do you mean?"

"I don't think it's a hard question. You want to be queen and that's why you're here. Not for me. Why?"

I don't know how to answer. The change in his tone surprises me.

"All right, let me make this easier." Edgar shifts, propping his hands on his thighs. "I asked my father to give this ball so I could find a wife. Do you want to know *why* I want another wife?"

"Y-yes," I think I'm expected to say.

"One," he says, "I need an heir. A son. Or let's just say, a *legitimate* son." He chuckles and winks at me. "Two, I want a beautiful woman to sit beside me on the throne. It looks good, you know? Three, my daughter needs a mother, one that can manage her. And given that little... dispute... I observed between you earlier, I think you have the spirit to rein her in. And four, well, I get lonely sometimes. Mistresses, sooner or later, must be sent back to their husbands. I want someone for me."

My heart has stopped crashing. It has become a lump of coal, dull and heavy. I feel that sickening sense of loss, like waking out of a beautiful dream. Knowing it's gone and you can't get it back.

"Now what do you want?" He's not even smiling now. This is a business deal. An exchange of offers as we weigh the mutual benefits. Fine. If that's how it is, I can play along.

"I have a stepmother and two stepsisters. I hate them. They have always been cruel to me. I want to become queen to rise above them, to prove myself better than they can ever be. And I want to punish them."

"Really?" Edgar laughs and it's not friendly. "I mean, that's all you've got? Petty revenge on your family? I guess I expected more. But sure, fair enough. As queen you can punish them any way you like. Crush every enemy you've ever had, if you so choose. That is what I can offer you. Are we in agreement?"

I look down at my hands. "I... I don't know." I didn't like his talk of mistresses. If he's had them before, he'll have them again. And I know the rules that *men* have made. Infidelity is only a woman's crime. He will expect me to be loyal while he runs around freely. That isn't me. If I choose to, I can be faithful, but I want the same in return.

I rise to my feet. "Thank you, Prince Edgar, for your generous offer. I will give it some thought and-"

Edgar laughs and stands with me. "Look up there." He points to the tower behind us, to a small, dark window tucked high in the curving wall. "Let's go up, shall we? That window commands a lovely view of the kingdom. And I think... when we're alone... I can convince you that you'll like me as a husband."

One thing I have learned: when a man invites you into a private room with him, it is not to enjoy *the view.* That quick, I don't like Prince Edgar. He is not like Papa. I didn't know until now that I wanted someone like Papa. Someone to love me, not use me.

I stand straighter. "No, Your Highness, I would like to stay here. Perhaps we can walk in the garden."

Edgar, still smiling, wraps his fingers around my arm. A tight, commanding hold. "We're going up first."

Impulsively, I kick his shin with the toe of my crystal slipper. He flinches, baring his teeth, but does not release my arm. Then he laughs.

"You see?" He tugs me closer. "The moment I saw you, I knew you were perfect for me. I knew that black dress meant a soul even blacker. You are-" he slides a finger down my cheek "-everything I have ever desired."

Then he strikes me across the face.

The blow knocks me over and my hands hit the stone slabs of the terrace. I crouch on the ground, too shocked to cry out, my mouth open wide. Never, never have I been struck. Not even by Stepmother. My cheek tingles and I felt a hot slice when his hand hit my cheekbone. I touch the spot and find blood on my fingertips. A cut from his wedding ring.

I'm shaking. Edgar crouches beside me, hands resting on his knees. "My offer of marriage," he says in a low, cutting voice, "was merely a courtesy. Do not think for a moment that you have a choice. You are my bride, little crow. Now stand up and tell me your name."

I'm still too shocked to move. My thoughts fly like bats in a cave, whirling, screeching. I remember that Moody once courted a man, a man who seemed nice. But she ended it suddenly and I didn't know why until I overheard Stepmother talking to her late at night. "You can be sure of one thing," Stepmother said, "If a man hits you once, he will hit you again. And again and again and again. Have nothing to do with such a man. Ever."

I do not want to be hit for the rest of my life.

"Are you having trouble obeying me?" Edgar grabs my arms and wrenches me upward. "Let me make something clear, darling. As my wife you will do *exactly* as I say." He shook me when he said 'exactly'. "And that includes having sons. Do not fail me in this as my last wife did."

"D-did she?" I gasp out. His grip is so hard. I don't know what to do.

"Sadly," he says. "The birth of our daughter was dangerous, both of them nearly died. The physicians told me my wife would never have another child. Such a pity - I really did like her. But she was no longer useful, you know? Let us hope you can do better. I would hate to have to clip your wings."

He killed his wife. Oh Papa! Papa, help me! I wriggle and flail but Edgar is too strong. He drags me to the door of that horrible tower while whispering soothing words in my ear, as if I'm a child having a tantrum. I scream but he claps a hand on my mouth and crushes me against his chest. I try to bite his hand but his fingers are clamped around my jaw. He knows what he's doing - he's done this before.

"Edgar? Edgar is something wrong?"

The voice – a woman's voice – comes up to us from the garden staircase. I feel Edgar's grip slacken instinctively.

"It's nothing, Mother!" he calls. "No need to-"

I slam my elbow into Edgar's stomach and wrench out of his grasp. The distraction gave me the moment I needed. I grab my skirt and run, as hard and as fast as I can. Across the terrace, down some stairs, around a corner, under an archway. I don't know where I'm going, except away. Away from him.

From somewhere high above the castle, I hear the long, heavy tolls of a clock striking midnight.

Chapter 18

I turn another corner and find myself at the front of the castle. I hear pounding steps from behind that tells me Edgar is chasing. *Papa help me!* He is the wolf now and I am the rabbit.

The terrace is too high for me to jump, I need the stairs. They're not far ahead, another thirty yards or so. The tall, double doors pour out their golden light. The two guards stand calm and quiet on either side, as if the world didn't just become a living nightmare.

I reach the staircase and hurl myself down it. My crystal slippers hammer the steps - *clink! clink! clink! clink! clink!* - fast as the tripping of my heart. I spy a team and carriage on the gravel drive below me – my carriage! Waiting for me just as I asked. Bless you, mouse-driver! Bless you forever and ever and always!

And then my foot turns under me and I fall.

I'm going too fast to stop. I tumble heavily, arms over legs, the hard edges of the stairs slamming my back, my hips, my shins. I roll to a stop near the bottom of the stairs, my skirt bunched over my knees. I've lost a shoe. Flash quick, I whip off the other shoe and sprint to the carriage on my bare feet. The mouse-driver quietly holds the door and I leap inside.

"Drive! Drive!" I shriek. "There's a cat!"

I'm right in guessing he would understand this. He springs up to the driver's seat and the carriage jerks forward, the horses jumping into full gallop. I'm kneeling on the floor, my whole body a throbbing bruise, peering over the edge of the window.

Edgar is at the bottom of the stairs. He's holding something white and shiny in his hand – my crystal slipper. He lifts it high as my carriage barrels away, his voice ringing out over the night.

"Do not think you can fly, little crow! I will find you!"

Chapter 19

We make it about one mile before the spell is broken. I just eased my sore body up onto the seat and peeked out the window. We're in the middle of a forest, still part of the king's land. Then the carriage groans and shudders. A few pumpkin seeds fall onto my skirt. When I look up, the ceiling has become soft and pulpy, flecked with pale seeds. With a wet, squishy sound, the walls begin to shrink around me.

I kick the door open. I do not want to die being crushed inside a pumpkin.

I throw myself out and hit the ground tumbling, the earth pounding my new bruises. Groaning, I push myself up to sitting and notice my dress is now the simple gray I always wear. A short distance ahead, the carriage is shrinking fast, losing its details. My rats scuttle toward me, no longer horses. And I catch the barest glimpse of the mouse before he darts into the forest, probably still thinking a cat is after us. Poor little mouse. Thank you. May you live a long and prosperous mouse-life.

Slowly, stiffly, I manage to stand up. The forest is quiet, other than noisy night bugs. I listen but hear no distant shouts or thunder of galloping hooves. I don't think Edgar is chasing me now.

Bending down, I hold out my hands. "Come here, boys." My rats crawl into my palms and I tuck them against my chest. I have a long, weary, barefooted walk ahead of me. But at least I'll have company.

I've hobbled only a few steps when the moon glints off something near the pumpkin. Oh no, NO! My slipper! Why didn't it disappear? Did Godnutter want to leave me a souvenir of my disastrous night? That sounds like her sick sense of humor. But... she didn't know how this would end. She only sensed it and warned me not to go.

I didn't listen.

Sobs rumble up in my throat but I choke them down. I don't want to be heard, just in case. My whole body is shaking. I feel like I just crawled out of a hole in the earth, lucky to be alive. I desperately want someone to hold me, comfort me, tell me it was all a bad dream. But I have no one.

What a horrible man. Who knew our prince could be such a monster? A few must know, probably some unfortunate girls like me. His daughter will likely grow up as cruel and vicious as he is. No, I am lucky to escape that family. Even my stupid steps are not as bad as they are.

The gravel is sharp beneath my feet. The black treetops slide over me, leaves whispering together. I move to the side of the road and try walking on weeds. But they're too long and tangly.

He'll forget about me. I'm only one girl and his kind is easily distracted. He might search for a while because he's mad I got away, but he'll get bored. I'm so glad I didn't tell him my name.

But as I stumble through that depressing wood, the rats and slipper growing heavy in my arms, I almost want to laugh.

I never thought I'd meet someone even badder than I am.

Chapter 20

"Cinderella."

I open my eyes, instantly conscious that my feet are in agony. Late morning glows white at my window and Stepmother stands near my bed, cold as uncooked meat.

"It was you," she says quietly. "I can't imagine how I failed to recognize you. But just as we were leaving, I realized-"

"Stepmother!" I spring off the bed and fall against her soft chest. "Stepmother, hold me, I'm so scared!" I squeeze her arms and whimper into the lacey front of her gown.

"Heavens, child, what's the matter?" She sounds more curious than sympathetic.

I tell her what happened. I leave out the magic stuff (like Godnutter) and say the black dress belonged to my mother. I tell her how the prince treated me. That doesn't seem to surprise her as much as the offer of marriage.

"He truly asked you to be his queen?" she says.

"Do you think he'll look for me?" I ask, pulling her sleeves. "Do you think he'll find me?"

Stepmother looks over my head, thoughtful. "Without knowing your name, it will be difficult. I suspect he'll lose interest."

I sniff and try nestling into her. She puts a firm hand on my shoulder and pries me off. "Well, thank goodness it's over. Now dry your face and come lay the table for breakfast." She turns stiffly and heads down the attic stairs.

I rub my face with my hand. Stepmother is about as comforting as a porcupine. But like she said, at least it's over.

Then a sudden thought grabs hold of my throat.

Is it over? I limp over to the small, square mirror on my wall. Godnutter said if I failed to win the prince, I would turn back into ordinary Cinderella. But the face in the mirror is still pretty Cinderella. Which means that the prince still wants me.

Which means it's not over.

No! I'll hide. I'll stay indoors for months if I have to. At least in this I can trust Stepmother. The last thing she'd want is for *me* to become queen. She'll lock me in the attic before she ever lets that happen.

The prince will give up. He has to, all he's got is my shoe. And whoever heard of finding someone with just a shoe?

Chapter 21

Nothing happens for a whole week. Everything feels the same: I do my chores; Stepmother barely speaks to me; Loony rages about how ugly I looked at the ball. This, I know, comes from jealously. Even though the prince turned out to be a weasel, she's still furious he wanted me and not her. Stupid pig. I *wish* he wanted her!

I check the mirror often but my beauty doesn't fade. I wish I had white magic to change something, make myself fat and pimpled, at least for a while. But the decanter is empty, locked back in my cupboard upstairs. And my nerves have made me snappish, if my chores earned any white magic all, I lost it right away.

And I won't call on Godnutter, absolutely not. She's a sneaking traitor. Wasn't the white magic supposed to make my life *better?* She's probably cackling somewhere in a cloud of smoke. If I ever see her again I'll shove that pipe through her ears.

It is Moody, finally, that drops the axe. I'm scrubbing a muddy footprint out of that wretched white carpet in the sitting room while she lounges on the couch, pretending to read a book. She flips a page and speaks without looking at me.

"He's looking for you, you know."

I stop scrubbing because my arms just turned to lead. "H-how – how do you know?"

"It's all over the kingdom." She turns her dull eyes and there's no pity there, not a drop. But the fact she's telling me at all must mean she feels something.

"Word's gone out that the prince is madly in love with the mysterious woman from the ball. He won't rest until he finds her. He is personally visiting every house in the kingdom and making all the young maidens try on that glass shoe. It's nuts."

"It was a crystal slipper," I murmur. My hand is still clamped around the scrubbing brush, my fingers wet. This can't be happening.

"He thinks the shoe will help him find her. It is uncommonly small."

Curse you, white magic. Curse you Godnutter for giving it to me. And curse myself for being so stupid. I'm about to become the prince's prisoner because of my freaking feet!

"Been going on for several days now." Moody turns back to her book.

I stand up, drying my hand on my skirt. "Thank you," is all I can say. I need to get to the attic, do some hard thinking. Maybe I can leave for a while, run off to another kingdom. I don't have any relatives to stay with but I could work in a tavern somewhere. Taverns always seem to want pretty girls.

I reach the door and look back. "Do you know where Stepmother is? I need to speak to her for a minute."

"Oh, don't do that," Moody says dryly. "She's trying to help him find you."

Chapter 22

I whirl around in the doorway. *"What?"*

Moody shrugs. "You know how she is. She doesn't like you much, but a queen in the family is a good thing. It'll mean more money, more prestige for the rest of us. She even wrote a letter."

"She wrote a letter!"

"Lunilla took it to the palace yesterday. Of course she read it on the way. Mother told the prince your name, described what you look like, and told him where we live. But I wouldn't worry."

I'm clutching the doorframe, my body a seething flame of fury. "Why not?"

"Because *every* mother wants the prince to choose her daughter. Lunilla says they're all making fools of themselves, claiming *their* daughter was the woman in black. He's probably received a thousand such letters." Moody shrugs again. "Just thought I'd tell you because you haven't been out."

I'm still holding the scrubbing brush in my hand. Now I hurl it at Moody. It strikes her shoulder, making her flinch and jump off the couch. "What was that for!" she shouts.

"Because you're useless!" I scream.

I turn down the hallway and see Loony coming toward me. She smirks and lifts her eyebrows like she wants to say something snarky. But I don't let her.

"Where is Stepmother?" I reach out and roughly grab her ear, digging my fingernails into the lobe. "Where is she?"

"Ow. OW! Stop it!" Loony shrieks, her head tilting against my hand. "She's in her room, get OFF me!"

I let go and sprint upstairs while Loony shouts "Freak!" and "Maniac!" and threatens to smash my head with a frying pan. I dash down the hall to Stepmother's bedroom and shove open the door without knocking. Stepmother is at her writing desk, scratching a quill over parchment.

"Writing to the prince again?" I snarl.

Stepmother looks up at me, then down at the parchment again. "No. Next week's menu for Cook." She dips the quill in the inkbottle and writes another line. "Who told you?" she asks quietly.

"Melodie." I'm shaking all over. I want to do so many things to her, each one worse than the next.

Stepmother sets down the quill and turns to me in her chair. She folds her hands in her lap. "I think perhaps you fail to consider the advantages of this match."

I point at her face. "Don't even try that. We both know that's not why you're doing it!"

Stepmother opens her hands. "Tell me, then. Why am I doing it?"

"Because you hate me. You've *always* hated me. You want the prince to find me so I'll be unhappy!"

Stepmother stands and paces a little, holding her elbows. She looks down at the floor as if thinking before she speaks.

"When your father came to court me, I admit I was happy. He spoke of you frequently, but I did not perceive you as a problem then. It wasn't until after we married...." She stops and takes a deep breath. "I saw the way he cherished you, how his eyes shone when he looked at you. They never shone for me. And then one day I realized the truth. He didn't marry me for me. He married me for *you*."

I silently disagree. Yes, perhaps that was part of it. But I do think my father cared for Stepmother. Not as much as he loved my mother, at least I hope not. But he wouldn't have married her unless he had some regard. My father was a good man.

But there's no point trying to convince her of that. She allowed her mind to warp the past, by now it's far beyond repair. And I couldn't care less.

"So you want to get rid of me," I say.

"Oh, much more than that, my darling." Stepmother says, her voice hardening into steel. "I want you to walk in my shoes, to marry a man who cares nothing for you except as a mother for his child. I want you to suffer as I have suffered."

I clench my fists. "Do you *think* I have not suffered?" My chest starts to heave. "You could have chosen to love me! I needed you when my father died, but you cast me away! If you had just been the mother I needed, I - I might have...."

"It would have made no difference. You were always a bad piece of work."

Tears flood up in my eyes. She still has the power to hurt me. "Maybe," I choke out, "some people turn bad because they have no one to love them."

Sniffling, I back towards the doorway. "And you won't succeed, you know. I'm leaving, right now. I'm going far away where the prince can't find me. And there's nothing you can do about that."

Stepmother looks at me, then past me. "Go ahead," she says. But I get the sense she's not talking to me.

When I turn to look, something heavy strikes the side of my head. I feel myself falling as the world goes black.

Chapter 23

I wake up in Stepmother's bed. My head feels heavy and swollen. With a low groan, I elbow myself up. My ankle is tied to the post of her bed with a thin rope, so tightly that my bare foot is puffy and red. I lean forward and start picking the knot with my fingernails.

"Don't do that or I'll have to hit you again."

I turn. Loony is sitting on a chair near the bed, holding onto a cast iron frying pan. So that's what she hit me with. Funny, I didn't think she was serious.

I sink back onto the pillow and shut my eyes. My head really hurts. "Where's Stepmother?"

"Out, trying to find the prince. By the way, *what* is that?" She points to the table beside Stepmother's bed. My crystal decanter sits on top, empty and twinkling.

I lunge at it but the rope stops me. Loony laughs and slides the decanter further down the table. "What is it?" she asks.

"You were in my room!" I shout.

"All over it," Lunilla says. "Me and Mother. She dumped out the drawers while I took an axe to that cupboard of yours. We really thought we'd find something much more interesting besides an empty bottle. What's it for?"

"Nothing," I snap.

Loony crosses her broad legs and smiles. "Don't worry, we'll figure it out. We were looking for something you wore to the ball, like the dress, some kind of proof. I mean, what'd you do, throw it in the river? Anyhow, Mother came down here and pulled off your loafers. She's taking them to the prince to show him the size of your feet."

They didn't find my crystal slipper? I remember kicking it under the bed the night I staggered in from the ball. That would have been fabulous proof. Good thing they're stupid, I guess.

I shrug. "He'll think they're for a child."

"Maybe. Maybe not. But it's worth a shot, right? And hey, we're in luck! The prince is searching our town today, so Mother shouldn't have to go far."

I dive back to the knot on my ankle. Loony smirks and raises the frying pan. "He can find you much easier if you're unconscious."

"Lunilla, please. Please, let me go!"

Loony settles back in her chair, smug as a cat. "You know, when you marry the prince, can you imagine what that will do for *me*? And my marriage chances? I'll be the queen's sister!"

"*Step*sister!" I spit out.

Loony hoists her foot up on the bedframe. "'Course I'd rather be queen myself. But if the prince is really the rat you described, well, sounds like he's perfect for you! You always liked rats, didn't you?" She gives me a disgusted look.

I start to cry. I can't help it. I'm trapped, I can barely feel my foot, and I'm going to be handed to the prince like a pig on a platter. By the very people who are supposed to be my family.

"I – I'm sorry, Lunilla."

"What?" she looks at me like I'm crazy.

I cry into my curled hand. "I'm just sorry, that's all. I know you never liked me much, but I didn't give you much reason to. Did you ever like me at all?"

Loony's grimacing like she smells something bad. "Oh, a little bit at the beginning. I guess."

"How did we lose that?" I wipe my wet eyes. "We could have been friends. I should have tried harder but I let hate get the better of me. And now look at me." I sniff loudly. "I always thought you had good stature. Good lungs too, you should try singing."

Loony is still scowling. "If you *think* that'll make me let you go-"

"I don't." I wipe my wet eyelashes. "I guess I just want you to know.

Loony rolls her eyes. As they reach one side, she notices the bedside table. She stares for a moment, then gasps.

My crystal decanter is alive with light, sparkles bouncing on the inside. When the sparkles dissolve, several drops of white liquid have collected at the bottom.

Chapter 24

"Melodie. MELODIE!" Loony jumps out of her chair and drops the frying pan. She skitters several feet back from the table, her eyes big and bulging.

"Huh?" I hear Moody's voice down the hall. She doesn't sound remotely interested in whatever Loony's screaming about.

"Come here! Quick! Quick!"

Moody doesn't come quick, but she comes. She slouches against the doorframe and doesn't look at me once. I guess she's not over the scrubbing brush incident.

"Look at this! Look!" Loony grabs the decanter and prattles about what happened. "It just appeared, like - like magic!"

Moody frowns and takes the decanter. She peers at the little blob of liquid inside. "Are you sure? It looks like spit."

"No! I saw it! The whole bottle glowed and then that stuff was in there!" Loony points at me. "She's a – she's a witch! She's got magic! I bet that's how she got to the ball! I bet that's why we didn't recognize her!" Loony flies at me and grabs my shoulder. "What is that stuff? Tell me now!" She shakes me roughly.

Meanwhile, I'm sitting here and cursing myself for apologizing to Loony. I wasn't trying to earn white magic! Everything I do comes back to spit in my face, like hot oil out of a pot.

"Tell me!" Loony shakes me again.

"That won't work, she's stubborn," Moody says. "We should take this to Mother."

"Wait – maybe we can test it!" Loony snatches the decanter from Moody and whips off the stopper. She sniffs the bottleneck carefully. "It smells fruity!" She opens her palm and tilts the bottle into it.

"Don't!" Moody pushes the bottle upright. "We don't know what it can do! You could turn into a chicken or something!"

"In that case, Cindy would be a chicken."

"It won't do anything for *you*," I growl. "It was meant for me and it will only work for me. There's not enough in there to do much of anything."

"But what does it do?" Moody asks.

I try to think of something scary. The magic will turn me into a wolf that can swallow them whole. Or something boring; the magic is just a fancy cure for stomachache. But it doesn't matter what lie I would've told because we all hear the snap of a downstairs door and Stepmother's voice calling out. "Lunilla! Melodie! Come here, my darlings, we have a special guest!" The jubilation in her tone can mean only one thing.

Prince Edgar is here.

Chapter 25

My stepsisters leave. The decanter goes with them. I wrestle with the knot on my ankle but panic has made me clumsy. My fingers fumble, too scared to slow down.

"Please – please!" I whisper. I have to escape now! But the knot does not slide and my fingernails shred. Through the murmur of conversation downstairs my ears pick out a man's voice, soft and pleasant, and my heart jumps right in my throat. I have to get out! I don't want to think of what Edgar might do if he finds me alone and tied to a bed. No, no, no....

I hear a soft scuffling by the wall and snap toward the sound. One of my rats! Stepmother and Loony ransacking my room must have scared him out. He pauses and looks up at me as if asking if I'm all right.

"Toil! Come here!" I wave him over, desperately happy. "Can you chew through this rope on my ankle? They trapped me."

Toil doesn't hesitate. He springs onto the side of the bed and claws his way up. It takes him only a minute to chew through the knot on my ankle.

"Thank you, darling!" I slide my hand over him, flattening his silky fur. Then I peel the rope off my ankle where it leaves purplish dents in my flesh. My foot tingles as blood begins to flow again.

I hurl myself off the bed and out of the room. I have no time to pack. It means leaving barefooted with the clothes on my back, but what choice do I have? I will not marry that cheater, beater, murderer.

I creep down the narrow back staircase that Cook uses. I'm near the kitchen now. A long corridor leads to the front of the house where the immaculate white sitting room is. I hear Stepmother speaking. "She'll be down shortly, she just wanted a few minutes to get ready. Lunilla, why don't you go and fetch her?"

I shouldn't have waited. I dash into the kitchen, planning to slip out the back door. But the room is dark and in my haste I kick the coal scuttle sitting by the stove. It clatters across the floor and hits the wall with metallic fanfare. I don't *believe* this!

"Cook?" I hear Loony say.

"Cook is out!" Stepmother's voice is sharp as a battle cry. She knows who's in the kitchen.

I wrench open the back door and spring out to the yard. It looks the same as the night I prepared for the ball, except now the pumpkins are gone, stored away in the cellar. I dash across the courtyard, hoping to reach the street beyond. There I have a chance of losing myself among the alleys.

No such luck. The back door bangs open and moments later Loony crashes against my back, toppling me onto the cobblestones. I land with her arms under my stomach and the air is punched right out of my lungs.

Pain. Pain. My mouth is wide open, trying to pull in air that won't come. My chin is scraped against the stones. After several seconds I wheeze out, "G-get off me!" But Loony is bigger, heavier, bulkier. She simply laughs in my ear. "Not a chance, sister."

I wriggle but it's like being under a cow. I hear commotion behind me, more running feet. Loony is warm on my back but the ground feels cool below me. I can't hear much with her breath in my ear, but the noises soon settle. And then, with soft, steady clops, a pair of shiny black boots steps in front of my face.

"Hello, little crow."

Chapter 26

It's him.

I can't see his face but his voice slides into me like a dark spell. My heart deadens. My limbs lose the will to move. There is no hope for me now, none at all.

"Release her," Edgar says and Loony lifts off me. Edgar crouches and takes careful hold of my arms. I allow him to lift me but I keep my eyes down. I don't want to look at him.

"It is you, my little crow, is it not?" He says it as tenderly as if we're long-estranged lovers. Hooking a finger under my chin, he gently tilts my face up to his. "Look at me," he whispers.

So I look. Oh my goodness, he's beautiful. His blue eyes are so soft and loving they remind me of Papa's. He's wearing a black suit tonight, a silver crown in his hair. He smiles gently and sadly, as if my absence pained him, and I even see tears in his eyes.

"It's you." He touches my cheek with his fingertips. "I have searched the kingdom, night and day, hoping to find you. I almost despaired." He grins now, a grin of heartfelt delight. "You're as beautiful as I remember."

My heart is aching, bleeding tears. If only he was really like this! But I know the real him, this is a performance. And we have an audience. Stepmother and Loony and Moody stand a few yards away, spaced around us like sentinels. And from the corner of my eye I notice two soldiers that must have come with the prince. Well, if Edgar can pretend, then so can I.

I shake my head. "I don't know you, sir."

Edgar smiles and takes hold of my hands. "Don't be shy, my dearest. How could I forget those eyes! You look less grand than when I last saw you, but your sweetness cannot be hidden. I've missed you so."

Oh, he's good. He's got Loony and Moody completely fooled, they both gaze at him hungrily. And Stepmother – her thin eyes shift from Edgar to me, not knowing who to believe. I can tell she doesn't like the way he's talking to me.

I lower my eyes. "I'm sorry, sir, but I do not know you. I am just a servant here."

"She's lying," Stepmother says. Edgar holds up a hand. "She is just being modest. One of the many things I admire about her. But don't worry. I have something to settle the question. Something she lost on the night of the ball." He turns and beckons to one of the soldiers.

The soldier is a young fellow with a hard, square jaw, thrust forward to convey his toughness. He looks misplaced in this yard full of women, with his belt and sword and pointed helmet. He approaches Edgar with a silver box not much bigger than... my foot. I know what will be inside.

Edgar takes the chest and tilts back the lid. And there it is, my crystal slipper. Nestled in a cushion of blue velvet and twinkling like a star. It's beautiful. But to me it's like the sack they slip over your head just before the executioner drops his blade.

Edgar carefully scoops out the shoe and hands the chest back to the soldier. I take a step back. "I will not put that on."

Edgar laughs good-naturedly. "What is there to fear? If you are not the girl I seek then the shoe will not fit you. And I'll leave you in peace. Here, slip it on." He lifts the shoe in both hands like an offering.

I step back again. "No." But darn it, I didn't notice that Loony moved to stand behind me. Her big hands grip my arms just above the elbows. "Royal decree, honeybee," she croons. "All maidens must try on the slipper. Even Melodie and I tried to wear it. But it's so ridiculously small. Just like your feet, isn't that funny?"

Edgar steps closer, still holding out the slipper. And now I can't move back. So I do the only thing I can think of: I swing up my foot and kick the underside of his hands. It works. The slipper shoots up, arches over his head, strikes the stone surface of the courtyard. And shatters.

I allow myself to smile. My slipper is ruined, smashed into sparkling fragments like diamonds. Only the long, thin heel remains intact, lying on the ground like an icicle.

I smirk at Edgar. "Oops. Silly me."

He's angry. His face has gone iron cold. I'm seeing the real Edgar now, the snake coiled to spring. He may carefully conceal his true nature before others, but the venom shows in his eyes. If my stupid steps were not present, I know he would hit me again, hard.

"Oh, don't worry about that," Moody says. "I've got the other slipper right here."

Edgar whirls around. Moody stands a few feet behind him, holding my left slipper. I don't believe it. Her face is glum as ever as she hands it to the prince. Like none of this matters to her.

All I can do is stare at her, shocked. She shrugs at me. The shrug is very telling, it says, 'Look, I tried to help you but you threw a scrub brush at me. We're done.'

I never liked her anyway.

"Well!" Edgar laughs as he takes the new slipper. "Aren't you full of surprises! Where did you get this?"

Moody points a finger at me. "In her room, the morning after the ball. I went in to speak with her and she was dead asleep on her bed, with bloody feet. The slipper was on the floor. I took it-" she glares at me "-so that Mother wouldn't find it."

"You what?" Stepmother cries.

Moody flicks her hand. "None of that matters now. Just put the shoe on and get rid of her."

The prince turns back to me, holding the shoe close to his chest this time. "Shall we, my dear?" He smiles like a hawk closing talons over its prey.

Loony's grip on me tightens. "Say the word and I'll hold her foot for you," she tells Edgar. I curl my fingers into claws. They won't take me down without a fight.

Edgar leans toward me but his smile falters. His knees twitch forward but he doesn't take a step. He looks down, frowning, and his knees twitch again.

"What's the matter?" Stepmother asks.

Edgar tries to laugh. "I – I can't move my feet!"

Stepmother frowns and shifts her weight forward. She gasps as her feet remain planted. "I can't either!"

I feel Loony's hands drop off me and she squeals like a piglet. "I just lowered my arms and I wasn't trying to!"

"It's her," Moody says, staring at me in awe. "She's using magic. I don't know how, but-"

"Witch! Witch!" Loony screams.

We all hear a laugh. A harsh, loud cackle that seems to come from nowhere. Everyone looks scared to death except me. I know that laugh.

"Oh, she's no witch," says a new voice to my right. "Just a selfish child. A vain little hussy. But she can't do magic - that's what I'm for."

The air beside me fills with color and shape and Godnutter appears before all of us.

Chapter 27

Still smoking! That blasted pipe is between her teeth and she grins around it. With her wrinkled dress and messy hair she looks like a mad woman that stumbled into our yard.

"All right, you can move now." She takes the pipe out of her mouth and wiggles the stem. A thin stream of sparkles flies out to each person. But if they *can* move now, they don't. Everyone – Edgar, Stepmother, Loony and Moody, the two soldiers – simply stares at Godnutter. They all look afraid, unsure of what to do or say.

Godnutter winks at Edgar. "Sorry, princey, no bride for you tonight. I'm the brat's fairy godmother and it's my job to look after her. I won't let you take her against her will."

Edgar does nothing but stare at her. Like me, he's probably heard tales of fairies but never saw one in real life. And he probably assumed they were pretty. But despite the white wings that sway open and shut like a butterfly's, Godnutter is just scary.

Stepmother finds her voice first. "Her... fairy godmother?"

"I was her ma's sister, once." Godnutter rocks on her feet like she's having a great time. "But that's a long story and not a cozy one either. In short, I'm in charge of the girl. Whether she deserves it or not, I'm here to protect her. And none of you can stop me."

"Are - are you the reason she went to the ball?" Moody asks carefully. "I thought she had a secret lover that helped her get there."

"Oh, she's had plenty of *those*." Godnutter rolls her eyes and Stepmother looks indignant. I guess she's mad she never knew that. "But yes, dearie, you're right about that. I gave her that hideous dress, and the slippers. She wanted the prince, foolish girl. But that's only because her family made her feel insignificant." Godnutter looks at Stepmother. "You did a lousy job, toots."

Stepmother lifts her haughty chin. "She was not my daughter."

"Yet she was a child entrusted to your care. And you let petty jealousy poison your heart. You rejected a little girl who just wanted to be loved and made her walk a path of loneliness. There are no words for that kind of cruelty. You utterly disgust me."

Stepmother's face is barely readable. Except for the tight clamping of her jaw, she shows no emotion.

Godnutter turns to Edgar who takes a reflexive step backward. "And you, well," Godnutter shakes her head sadly, "There's little hope for someone like you, a man who takes pleasure in harming women. But mark my words, princey, one day the world will see you for the beast that you are. And no one will pity you."

Edgar smirks but I can tell he's being cautious. Respectful of the power she wields. He probably doesn't want to be turned into a frog or something.

Godnutter steps over and wraps her arm around my shoulders. "Come, dear. I'm taking you away from these people. I can't give you much but I have a little cottage in a seaside village. You'll be safe there, you can start a new life."

A cottage by the sea. That sounds nice. Maybe I can set myself up as a dressmaker and find a nice man to marry. A new life, a new me.

But there's one more thing. "What about the white magic?" I ask. "Do I lose it?"

Godnutter chuckles. "You won the wager, dumpling. Our deal was that you'd lose the magic if you failed to win the prince. But look at him, he wants you desperately. The fact that you're turning him down is beside the point. No, the magic bottle is yours to keep. Those freaky good looks too."

"Is *that* how she got so pretty?" Stepmother asks bitterly. "I always knew it was something unnatural."

I can't help but gloat a little. "Yes, Stepmother. The more you mistreated me, the more magic I earned. I used it to improve my looks. So thank you! Your cruelty was useful to me."

Godnutter shoots a jet of smoke from her mouth. "That's enough, brat. It's time to go."

"Who has my decanter?" I ask, imperiously folding my arms. I know it came out here, I saw it, though my attention was mostly on the prince. Somebody was holding it. After several seconds of silence, Stepmother says, "Lunilla has it."

Lunilla is still behind me, so Godnutter and I turn to face her. But once I do, something hard smashes against the back of my head. I pitch forward as a shower of crystal rains down around me. I hit the ground, the white fragments bouncing and mixing with those left by the slipper. My crystal decanter. Stepmother threw it at me.

Pulsing waves of pain wash the back of my head. I'm breathing heavily through my nose. The white magic! The only thing of value I owned. Besides Papa, nothing else ever made me feel special. It was the decanter that generated the magic, I know this. A magical artifact, rarely bestowed. I will not be getting another.

"Well, *that* was uncalled for!" Godnutter barks.

"Keep quiet!" Stepmother shouts. I hear her footsteps approach me. "Sneaky little slug," she hisses. "So many secrets. Well! I've got a few of my own. Did your precious Papa ever talk to you about your *mother*?"

"Don't!" Godnutter says sharply.

"You will let me speak!" Stepmother snaps. "There's a reason he never spoke of her. Because she was wicked. She cared nothing for your father and broke his heart by fooling with other men.

They were like trinkets to her, her collection of lovers. And oh, how proud she was! When your father objected, she laughed at him."

My head feels swollen, too heavy to lift. I'm lying on my side, Godnutter before me, Stepmother behind. I squint up at Godnutter. "Is it true?"

Godnutter takes a long draw from her pipe. When she sighs, the smoke sprays out of her nostrils. "Our family has problems."

Lunilla snickers.

"He wanted me to *help* you," Stepmother goes on. "Teach you to be pure and kind and as unlike your mother as possible. But look at you." She pokes my shoulder with the toe of her shoe. "Just as much of a tramp as she was. It's a good thing your father *is* dead."

My eyes focus on the broken bits of crystal spread across the ground. The severed heel of my slipper is within reach. I thought it was intact but now I see a section broke off the tip, giving it a jagged point. I reach out and close my hand around the heel. "Don't you talk about my father," I growl. I spread my other hand on the ground and push up onto my knees.

Stepmother laughs. "Why not? He was no prize. A man of moderate wealth at best. His only treasure was his *daughter.*" Stepmother grinds out the word like a curse. "But take no pride in that, my darling. When he was dying, he confided to me that because of your mother's wicked ways, he was never even sure if you *were* his daughter."

A high shriek breaks out of me. I spring off my knees, thrust upward with my hand, and the sharp heel punctures Stepmother's stomach. She makes a hard sound - "uh!" – and bends over me, wide-eyed. Grunting, I shove my hand against her and bury the crystal spike in her body.

Loony and Moody scream as Stepmother drops. Now she is on the ground and I'm standing above her. She's making unpleasant gasps, her whole body jerking. Then, like a clock winding down, her motions slow before settling into silence.

Chapter 28

Nobody moves. Nobody speaks. They all stand there and stare at me, waiting....

I stare at Stepmother. My chest lifts and falls, lifts and falls, breaths quickening rather than slowing. I just killed my stepmother. Someone that moments ago was moving and speaking and blinking. Now she looks like a fallen branch, arms poking out, eyes blank. Blood is pooling through the front of her dress, staining it black. She was alive and now she's dead. Dead forever.

From the corner of my eye, I detect motion. Godnutter is slowly shaking her head. When she looks at me, I feel her emotions as if they were my own. Shame. Sorrow. Pity. Her eyes have become a sea of sunken hopes.

"I wanted to spare you this," she says. "But I failed... and so did you. I'm sorry, my child. I cannot help you anymore."

And just like that, she's gone.

"Wait!" I throw out my hand. But nothing remains of my fairy godmother except a drifting tendril of smoke. I feel like the wind was knocked out of me again.

And then Edgar laughs. He claps his hands together in slow, mock applause. "Beautiful!" He strolls toward me with a proud smile. "Must say, it's quite fun to witness a murder. Better than theater, you know? Didn't I say you were perfect for me?"

I glare at him through my tears. "Leave me alone!"

Edgar steps close to me, dropping his voice to a murmur. "Where will you fly to now, little crow? There is nowhere you can go, except the gallows. Murder is a hanging offense, you know."

I do know. My mouth goes dry as ashes.

Edgar pokes out his lower lip, pretending to feel sorry. "Whatever shall we do? I don't want you to die. So... how about this? If you accept my offer of marriage and come quietly, I *might* be able to smooth this over. I am the prince, after all."

"What!" Loony shouts. She stomps over to us, her red cheeks slick with tears. "She just killed my MOTHER! She has to die NOW! Tonight!"

"We'll do it ourselves, if you don't," Moody says. She isn't crying but her face is sickly gray.

"Huh." Edgar strokes his chin and winks at me. "They're awfully troublesome, aren't they? What should we do with them, Crow?"

I look up at him

"It's your call, my queen."

I clamp my teeth together. "Lock them up!"

Edgar turns and nods at his soldiers. Immediately, they head for my stepsisters who gasp and flee from the yard. I hear them shrieking as the soldiers pursue them out to the street.

"How nice. Now we can talk." Edgar smiles and cradles my cheek with his hand. We're alone now – if you don't count my stepmother's carcass.

Edgar slides his thumb over the cut he made on my cheekbone. "What is your name?"

I close my eyes. "Cinderella."

"Really! I think I prefer Crow. Well – Cinderella – do you consent to be my wife?"

I don't want to go with him. But I know I have no choice. I am Edgar's prisoner now, bound by chains that I forged for myself. I must wear them bravely.

"Yes," I whisper.

Edgar tilts up my face and presses a soft kiss to my lips. It's a nice kiss. I suspect this is how Edgar will be, a dove one moment, a wolf the next. I will have to get used to it.

"Now, just for formality's sake...." Edgar takes a step back and lifts my crystal slipper off the ground. He must have set it down while Godnutter was here.

I sigh and lift my skirt to mid-calf. Edgar bends on one knee and offers the shoe. I slip my toes inside the cool crystal, my heel settling down.

And of course, it fits perfectly.

Chapter 29

Edgar and I drive back to the palace. I can't see much outside the carriage window, just dark houses, dark pastures, dark trees. Edgar sits across from me, obscured in shadows, his foot raised comfortably on his knee.

"The wedding will be a week from today," he says.

I nod.

"And I think I would like it if you wore a black dress. It suits you, you know?"

I nod again. I will always wear black after this.

"After which, my mother will instruct you in your duties as princess. Nothing much, of course. Your biggest challenge will be my daughter."

I stop nodding. I forgot about the daughter.

"Tomorrow I'll let you have breakfast with her. I'll introduce you as her new mother, though she'll probably hate you for that. She's a stubborn girl but not without her charms. You will have to be firm with her, but loving, always loving. Is that clear?"

A new idea creeps into the back of my head. I resist the urge to smile.

"As for tonight, you'll sleep in the chamber formerly used by my wife. It'll be your room now. I think you'll like it, it's quite luxurious. You'll have plenty of freedom in your new life, most of the time I won't trouble you at all. But when I knock-" he looks right at me, "I expect you to let me in."

I smirk at him. "You won't be the first."

Edgar leans forward to pat my knee. "And you won't be the last. But we'll make a good team, Crow. You wait and see."

"What about my stepmother?" I ask.

"Oh, that was terrible wasn't it? Grabbing your throat just because I didn't choose *her* daughter as my bride? It's a good thing you had that spike in your hand or she would've strangled you right there!"

I sit back and smile. "That'll work."

"Ironic though, isn't it? Now you get to be a stepmother yourself. It's almost like your taking her place."

My insides curdle at the thought. I don't want to be a stepmother, especially not for that nasty little princess. She'll do her best to make my life hellish, that I know.

"What's your daughter's name?" I ask.

Edgar snickers. "It might seem odd to you. She was such a beautiful baby – hair black as ebony, skin white as snow. So we called her Snow White."

Chapter 30

Did I win? Did I lose? I honestly don't know. It's a twisted world, a world in which sometimes the worst thing that can happen to you is to get exactly what you want.

The wedding was lavish. Looked like the whole kingdom showed up to welcome me. I was presented to the people from outside the palace, on top of those circular stairs, and they looked like an ocean of heads. Here and there I recognized a face from my old neighborhood. The jealousy was delicious.

My stepsisters did not attend. They're being held in a remote tower prison until I decide what to do with them. I might make up my mind in a decade or two.

It's late now, close to midnight. I'm standing alone in my royal bedchamber, gazing into the mirror. I've got a new black dress that bares my shoulders, a new tiara with silver spikes. But no more crystal slippers. Those things are bad luck, I think.

The mirror is large and elliptical and framed in heavy gold. For some reason I feel better when I look inside it. Reassured, as if the mirror somehow knows me. I know it sounds weird, but even when I'm in other parts of the palace, I can still feel the mirror, calling me to stand before it.

My beauty – it's all I have now. But no more magic to keep it fresh. I miss the white magic. It gave me a sense of control. Still... there must be other forms of magic out there. Darker, more sinister kinds, perhaps. But I can learn them. I will find a way.

Edgar has hit me twice already, once on the morning of our wedding. But I know how to punish him now: through his daughter. She'll have her own wicked stepmother - and I learned from the best. I will ruin her life just as my stepmother ruined mine. It'll make Edgar furious, probably more violent. But I will have courage and be cruel.

She's worse than I thought, that Snow White. Too pretty for her own good. If I'm not careful she'll someday become even prettier than I am. And I rather enjoy being fairest in the land, having the admiration of the whole kingdom. I won't let her take that from me.

My reflection smiles, unworried. It's a new life now, new enemies to conquer. The old Cinderella is dead, she died the moment I plunged that spike into Stepmother. No longer will I subjugate myself to anyone, no longer will I take refuge in my memories of Papa. Try as I might, I no longer see myself as his daughter. Not just because of my mother's secret, but because I've taken a life. Somehow, that pushed my father far away, beyond my reach. I have no family left, no real identity. I will have to create it for myself.

My eyes meet those in the glass, blue and brutal. I lift my chin. "Mirror, mirror, on the wall. Who is the fairest one of all?"

I feel the aura of comfort coming from the mirror. And I know who I am.

I am the Evil Queen.

Coming Next:

Sneaky Snow White

Join the Mailing List to receive updates and alerts
when the next book is released.

http://www.anitavalleart.com/mailinglist.html

About the Author

I've sometimes wondered about Cinderella.
How could she stay so sweet and cheerful when
she gets nothing but abuse from her family? I
think even the most good-natured person would
become bitter and vindictive after a while. In this
story, I wanted to show a more wounded side of
Cinderella, the side that is hurting from being
unloved. Love brings out the best in people, but
hate brings out the worst.

So... about me: I live near Poughkeepsie, New
York with my husband, three boys, and no pets. I
have a hard time getting my boys to stop playing
video games and read more books. My house is

often a mess because I'm either out at my day job, or helping my kids with homework, or trying to squeeze in some writing and drawing. Yet I get frustrated when my house isn't clean. Other than strangers on the internet, I almost never tell anyone I know that I write books, because I have a weird insecurity that they won't take me seriously. But I never feel happier than when I'm working on my projects.

If you have a few spare minutes, would you do me a favor and write a review? That really helps to give the book credibility. Also, please consider checking out my other books. Most of the time, I'm working on *The Nine Princesses Novellas,* a fun series about a family of teenage princesses. I've tacked on a few chapters of *Maelyn,* the first story, if you'd like to try it out. You can download the whole book FREE from most major book sites.

Thanks so much for supporting an indie author. God bless you.

-Anita Valle

Maelyn

The Nine Princesses Novellas

Prologue

The child was too young to understand death. All she knew was that Mama would not move. The child prodded and whined and stomped her small feet. But nothing stirred Mama from her bed.

When the cottage darkened, the child slept on the floor rushes, collecting bits of dried grass in her brown hair. At dawn she rubbed her eyes with the backs of her hands and cried at the pain in her belly. She could speak the word "bread" but she could not find any.

She padded to the door and gripped the latch above her head. Without looking back at Mama, she ventured out in quest of bread.

Everything felt warm. The drying mud that clutched her toes; the breeze against her cheeks; the puddle of rainwater in which she dunked her face, gulping until it dribbled a dark streak down the front of her dress.

She wandered across the scant village, in and out of the scattered huts. No bread. No animals. No people either, except a few who slept like Mama.

In the last cottage she found half an apple and a wedge of cheese on a low sill. She devoured them on sight. The pain in her belly ebbed, but not enough.

Wandering out again, the child watched the stillness around her. She didn't understand the quiet, only the feeling of wrongness it gave her. So her small feet turned away from the village and carried her across fields of flat emptiness. She found a road and instinctively followed it, walking until her legs ached and the pain in her belly sharpened again.

When evening burned the sky pink as her sun-baked cheeks, she sat on the parched grass by the road and cried into the backs of her hands again. The sound of approaching horses meant nothing to her. Horses were not bread.

"Is that a child?" someone asked.

The child looked up at a very large man on a very large horse. He wore colors she'd never seen and things that sparkled like sunlight on water. She cried harder in fear of his strangeness.

"Yes, Sire. A girl, I think." A smaller man on a smaller horse rode by the shiny man. He too wore strange colors, but nothing that sparkled.

"Alone," said the shiny man, his eyes sweeping acres of nothingness behind her. "Must be from one of the stricken villages."

"None in the villages survived, my lord."

"None that caught the Fever survived. Clearly this girl did not catch it." He watched her for a long moment. "Fetch her, Dorian."

The child squealed and thrashed as she was carried to the shiny man and placed on his horse. "There now, little pet." The shiny man held her firmly, one arm circled around her middle. He dug through a satchel at his side and withdrew a small golden loaf.

The child stopped thrashing. "Bread!"

The horse beneath her moved onward. The shiny man carefully picked the rushes from her hair. But the child noticed neither as she crammed her cheeks with milk-white softness, richer, sweeter, more satisfying than anything she knew.

"Next town is not far, Sire," said the one called Dorian. "Shall we leave the girl there?"

With her belly quiet, heavy sleepiness took over. The child curled against the shiny man, cooling her face on his smooth tunic. She felt his hand rest atop her head; his fingers stroke her hair. Just before slipping under, she caught his soft reply.

"No. Not this one."

Chapter 1

Fifteen Years Later....

Princess Maelyn frowned at the royal messenger. "Rowan, you look terrible. Your face is red as fire."

"I *feel* terrible." Rowan grimaced and rubbed his forehead. "But no matter, my lady, it will pass. I've come with a message from your uncle, the High King of Grunwold."

Maelyn stiffened in her throne. She liked her uncle as much as she liked bandits in her bedchamber. Less. At least bandits could be hanged.

"He wants to know if the rumors are true," said Rowan.

Maelyn lifted her chin. "What rumors?" Though she already knew.

Rowan cast down his eyes, flawlessly respectful. "The rumors that you have dismissed every servant in the castle."

Maelyn did not even blink. "I have."

"The footmen?"

"Yes."

"The counselors?"

"Yes."

"Even your ladies-in-waiting?"

"*All* of the servants," said Maelyn, impatience crawling through her tone. "I expelled every one of them, from the sentries to the scullery maids. No one dwells in this castle but my sisters and myself."

Rowan nodded. "Very good, my lady. I will tell the king." Droplets gathered on his forehead and he yanked the cap off his gray hair to dab his face. "Beg your pardon, my lady.... May I ask why?"

"Did the king ask why?" Maelyn raised a single eyebrow.

"No," said Rowan.

"Then you may go." Maelyn unhooked her ivory cape and draped it on the arm of her throne. She felt anxious to reach her chamber and extract the combs bearing up her heavy brown hair. "Rest well before your journey, Rowan. Have you eaten?"

Rowan nodded, dabbing his face again. Maelyn noticed a trembling at his knees and sensed he struggled to stand erect. She hurried down the four steps that lifted her throne above her visitors.

"Come. I'll help you to your horse." She tucked herself under Rowan's arm, alarmed at the fierce heat coming from his body. "Lean on me."

She felt him settle against her shoulder. She intended to give him light support, but suddenly the full weight of his six-foot stature crushed down on her. Maelyn gasped as she crumpled to the marble floor with Rowan on top of her.

"Rowan!" Maelyn cried, uncertain whether to be outraged or terrified. He felt like a boulder on her ribs. His hot face pressed against her neck. She squirmed until she'd freed her hands and pushed back his head. His eyes....

Maelyn's shriek reached every corner of the castle.

Chapter 2

"People die too much," said Princess Coralina Corissa at breakfast.

Maelyn looked horrified. "Coco!"

"Tell me they don't!" Coralina challenged with her vivid purple eyes. "Every twelve seconds somebody drops. From plague or treachery or just stupidity. Can't they find something better to do?"

"Rowan wasn't stupid," said Arialain, the youngest princess. She drooped over her berries and porridge, her wispy yellow hair nearly dipping into the bowl. "He was kind.... Even when I was little...."

Maelyn nodded. It didn't surprise her to see Arialain so distraught. Her soft heart was easily touched. "He *was* kind. We've lost a faithful servant."

Coralina rolled her eyes theatrically. "We've lost *all* our faithful servants, remember?"

Maelyn bristled and dug her spoon into her own porridge. How little Coco knew. How little they all knew....

She flicked a glance at the other princesses seated at the table. Either Rowan's death had a quieting effect or they had given up arguing about the servants. Only Coralina seemed unaffected.

"Well, which was it?" Coralina asked.

"What?" said Maelyn.

"Plague, treachery or stupidity?"

Maelyn shut her eyes. "Red Fever." Without looking she could feel the startled eyes of her sisters. "I thought the realm was finally rid of it."

"Are you... are you sure?" Arialain asked.

Maelyn nodded. Rowan had probably woken in perfect health yesterday morning. By evening he was dead. That was Red Fever.

Coralina lifted a wedge of cheese off a silver platter and bit off the tip. "Who will carry our messages now?"

"No one, I hope," said Maelyn, and Coralina laughed. But Maelyn brightened with a new thought. No messenger meant no correspondence with her uncle, the High King of Grunwold. Rowan would not be returning to answer for the "rumors".

Hopefully the king wouldn't notice.

Chapter 3

When night blackened the castle windows, Maelyn turned the latch on her library door. She needed to be Maelyn for a while. Not the daughter of a king. Not the eldest of nine sisters. Not the ruling princess of Runa Realm. Just Maelyn and her books.

She had spent the day dutifully. Attended Rowan's burial. Gave his wife a satchel of goldens. Prayed with the friar. Sung with the minstrel. Spoken with eloquence of Rowan's faithful service. Ate the mutton pie served to her.

Maelyn sighed. She *was* grieving. But displaying grief as a duty was disheartening.

She lit a candle and gazed about her library, comfortably cluttered with padded reading chairs, miniscule tables, and towering shelves of books. She'd find a new story and steep her mind in another world.

She held her stub of candle at eye level and searched the nearest shelf for a book she hadn't read. *The Finicky Fairy* – that was fun, she'd read it last winter. *The Useless Unicorn.* A bit silly but animal stories were never her favorites. *The Carnivorous Carriage.* If books were any less scarce, she'd have burnt that one. It still gave her nightmares.

Her candle flame passed all the titles on the shelf, then the two shelves above. It glided to the next bookcase, brushing each book with its gentle light. Methodically, the flame worked its way across the walls, lighting shelf after shelf. Maelyn found herself murmuring the titles aloud. "*The Peculiar Prisoner, The Nauseous Knight, The Sinister Slippers*, aren't there any I haven't read?" Ten minutes of careful searching later, Maelyn faced the dismal truth – she was bookless.

Disgusted, she blew out her candle and stalked to the window, though night hung too heavily to see beyond the glass. This meant a walk into town and a wearisome haggle with the Book Miser.

She hated that man.

Chapter 4

"You can't be his younger brother," said Maelyn. "Rowan had only a sister."

"I was not born his brother," said the young man before her throne. "His mother took me in as a child."

"You were an orphan?" Maelyn asked.

"Yes, my lady. We have that in common."

Maelyn blinked, stunned at his boldness. Though all of Runa knew her birth story, no one spoke of it. Ever. "And what do they call you?" she asked to change the subject.

"Willow, my lady." The young man grinned. "The family is fond of trees."

Maelyn pinched her smile before it spread. The sister was Maple. The father was Spruce. Even Rowan's infant son had been called Lumen for the ancient trees native to Runa.

Still she felt suspicious. "Why have I never seen you before?" Though she'd noticed him at the burial, he looked too unlike Rowan to be taken for family. Slender and tall. Yellow hair in careless waves. Barely older than herself, she guessed.

"I don't venture out much," said Willow. "I work best in solitude."

"Yet you wish to be Royal Messenger?" Maelyn lifted her eyebrows. "That means venturing out quite a bit."

"I do wish it." Willow's face grew earnest. "My brother served as your messenger, and his father before him. It would honor me to do the same."

His voice rang true but Maelyn groaned inwardly. A new messenger meant her uncle's question must be answered. She wished she had another task for Willow, something to delay sending him to Grunwold....

Maelyn pressed her scepter to her lips for a long moment. "Willow... do you know the Book Miser who lives in Creaklee?"

Willow looked taken aback. "I – I do, my lady. I've dealt with him."

"Does he like you?"

Willow smirked. "Does he like anyone?"

Maelyn laughed, ashamed that she did. "I have your first task." She reached beneath the legs of her throne and withdrew *The Finicky Fairy*. "I'm in need of something new to read. Take this to the Book Miser and trade it for whatever he will give you."

Willow took the book from her outstretched hand and bowed. "My deepest thanks, my lady. I will not fail you."

He strode for the arched doors at the far end of the throne room. Maelyn relaxed in her chair. How perfect. Her uncle would receive no message. And she would gain a new book without a verbal tussle with that wretched miser.

Chapter 5

It was the messenger's fault.

If he hadn't revealed he was an orphan, she might be sleeping now. Not watching the shadowy folds of her bed curtains while her mind simmered with memories.

Maelyn pushed back the curtains and lit a candle on her bedside table. From a small drawer she removed a worn and tattered journal, lifting it with reverent fingers. She settled back in her pillows and opened to the first page. Her smile softened at the firm handwriting, comforting as the face of a friend.

Once there was a king so enchanted by his beautiful bride that he named his realm anew, calling it Runa in her honor.

The king gave his precious queen all her heart could ask, but one. She longed for a daughter. Nightly the couple prayed, but for nine years the nursery sat as empty as the queen's arms.

In their tenth year, a terrible fever struck the realm, bringing death to nearly every household. In desperation, the king journeyed to nine distant

*kingdoms in hopes of finding a cure. But like a
filthy cloak, the fever covered them all.*

*Before turning back, the king chanced upon a
small child, the sole survivor of her village. An idea
sprouted in his mind. He could not cure the fever,
but perhaps the hole in the queen's heart.*

*Months later the king returned home and
presented his astonished queen with not one, but
nine baby girls. "One from each kingdom I visited,"
said the king. "They are orphans."*

*The queen wept joyously at the row of cradles,
each bearing a sleeping infant. After bestowing a
kiss on each child's forehead she said, "Now they
are princesses."*

Maelyn returned her father's journal to the
drawer. She'd been the oldest baby in that row of
cradles – about three years of age when Father
found her by the road. Arialain had been less
than a week, frail and born too early. Nine girls
from nine kingdoms, orphaned by nameless
strangers. Suddenly they became sisters, bound
not by blood, but by their parents' love.

Maelyn slid out of bed, shivering as her feet
touched the floorboards. She wrapped a heavy
shawl over her nightdress and padded to the

window. The kingdom nestled in darkness thick as a wool blanket but the first smudges of sunlight colored the horizon.

She remembered only fragments of that distant day. Mama's dead face. The long road that blistered her feet. Her terror when Dorian, the king's manservant, lifted her off the ground. How good the bread tasted....

"You never saw us as orphans," she said, addressing her unseen father. "You called us 'hidden princesses'. Born in other lands, waiting for you to find us." Maelyn smiled weakly. "But Father, many do not see us this way. I never knew how many... until you were gone."

■ ■

<u>Books by Anita Valle</u>

Maelyn: The Nine Princesses Novellas –1

Coralina: The Nine Princesses Novellas –2

Heidel: The Nine Princesses Novellas –3

The Bully Monster

50 Princesses Coloring Book

The Best Princess Coloring Book

Dog Cartoons Coloring Book

For more information, please visit my website:

http://www.anitavalleart.com

or e-mail me: anitavalleart@yahoo.com

CPSIA information can be obtained
at www.ICGtesting.com
Printed in the USA
FSOW02n1945010616
21066FS